Paddy O'R
novels, a col
stories, and a novella. Her novels have been
shortlisted for major awards, and her stories
have been widely published, anthologised
and broadcast in Australia and overseas.

PRAISE FOR *THE END OF THE WORLD*
'*The End of the World* is an excellent collection: formally
adventurous, sharp-witted and beautifully crafted. Even
the minor pieces are written with polish and aplomb.'
Australian Literary Review

'Each O'Reilly story winks and coruscates with flashes
of intelligence and humour, insight and empathy …
The End of the World is fresh on every page, adventurous,
enlightening, nicely restrained yet vivid and often moving.'
Australian

'Read one beside the other, [the stories] mark out
the emotional and imaginative landscape of a writer of
real flair.' *Sydney Morning Herald*

'These are exceptional stories, full of imaginative and
evocative portraits of all sorts of people.' *Adelaide Review*

ALSO BY PADDY O'REILLY

NOVELS
The Wonders
The Fine Colour of Rust (as P.A. O'Reilly)
The Factory

SHORT STORIES
The End of the World

NOVELLA
Deep Water (in *Love & Desire*, ed. Cate Kennedy)

NON-FICTION
It Happened in a Holden (editor)

PERIPHERAL VISION

stories

PADDY O'REILLY

UQP

First published 2015 by University of Queensland Press
PO Box 6042, St Lucia, Queensland 4067 Australia

www.uqp.com.au
uqp@uqp.uq.edu.au

© Paddy O'Reilly 2015

This book is copyright. Except for private study, research,
criticism or reviews, as permitted under the Copyright Act,
no part of this book may be reproduced, stored in a retrieval system,
or transmitted in any form or by any means without prior
written permission. Enquiries should be made to the publisher.

Cover design by Design by Committee
Typeset in 11/16 pt Bembo Std by Post Pre-press Group, Brisbane
Printed in Australia by McPherson's Printing Group

National Library of Australia
Cataloguing-in-Publication data is available at http://catalogue.nla.gov.au

ISBN 978 0 7022 53607 (pbk)
ISBN 978 0 7022 55182 (ePDF)
ISBN 978 0 7022 55199 (ePub)
ISBN 978 0 7022 55205 (Kindle)

University of Queensland Press uses papers that are natural, renewable and
recyclable products made from wood grown in sustainable forests. The
logging and manufacturing processes conform to the environmental
regulations of the country of origin.

Contents

The Salesman

Marly sat on the front verandah, waiting. Shaun and Azza had been working on Azza's car all day, driving the ute to the wrecker's for parts, taking Azza's black V8 for spins around the streets, steering the big car back through the hole in the fence to bury their heads under the bonnet like stupid long-legged emus. It was past six o'clock, though you wouldn't know from the heat. The house was cooked. Even the fridge was moaning. Marly was desperate for a beer.

She leaned back in the verandah armchair and wiped the sweat from her face. Chances were that the boys had stopped in at the pub on their way home from Supercheap. They'd be standing at the bar, promising each other just one beer before they headed back. And that meant she was stuck. Shaun had insisted they rent this crappy house, miles from anything except other crappy houses, because it had a ready-made hoist and pit in the yard and he'd be able to make a few extra dollars fixing mates' cars. Six months later and all anyone had ever paid was a slab. A half-empty slab by the time the guy had driven off.

She pulled her phone from her pocket and played with the buttons. No credit. No one had texted or called. Out in the front yard the dog yawned and stretched out in the patch of dust he had claimed as his own when Shaun brought him back from the swap meet a couple of months ago. Marly didn't get the idea of a dog. They didn't do anything for you. They didn't do anything at all except eat and sleep and shit. Cable had chosen one corner of the yard for shitting, and it happened to be on the way to the letterbox. The rest of the yard was littered with things Shaun had been going to fix but had never got around to. They'd all ended up in front of the house, waiting for the big day when he'd load up the ute and head off to the tip. Except Marly knew from experience that a trip to the tip meant a trip to the tip shop. The amount of rubbish around the house stayed the same – it only changed in shape and degree of uselessness.

'Excuse me, madam, am I speaking to the mistress of the house?'

Marly shaded her eyes and squinted at the dark-skinned man standing beyond the fence. 'Whatever you're selling, we don't want it.'

The man was short and slender, with small hands holding a blue clipboard, and feet in shiny black shoes tied with neat bows. He shook his head.

'I am not a salesman, madam. I am not here to sell you a single thing.' His face was perfectly proportioned, like a doll's. His skin was a rich toffee colour. He had the eyes of a girl, runny brown with thick lashes and an upward tilt

2

on the outside. He was as beautiful as a girl. Maybe he was a girl. Marly had seen plenty of sex-change people on TV shows. He might once have been a girl and now he had turned into a beautiful man pumped full of hormones with a prick made of sewn-up bits of skin and flesh.

'Madam, I wonder if I might have a glass of water. I'm very tired, and thankfully this is my last street for the day, but I still have to walk through the reserve to get back to my car. It's very hot. Very hot indeed.'

She could see the sweat glistening on his upper lip. His white business shirt was stuck to his chest. What would be the harm?

'You can come and wait on the verandah in the shade and I'll get you some water. But don't you come near me,' Marly said, certain that this honey-dark man with his girl eyes would bewitch her somehow into kissing him. 'You sit on the steps there. My husband will be home any minute.'

As if he had heard her, Shaun's tune rang out from the mobile.

'Azza's shouting us pizza for tea. You want capricciosa?'

He was slack in plenty of ways, but no other boyfriend had been as attentive as Shaun. She would never do better than this – a man who thought about what she might want, who asked, who had not once in eleven months raised a hand to her.

'With double cheese and, hon, don't hang up – I've got no credit. There's a guy here, he wants to sell us …' She paused. What did the Paki want to sell them? He was sitting on the verandah steps in the shade, elbows on his knees, shirtsleeves rolled up and hands hanging to his ankles. The blue clipboard and a canvas shoulder bag she hadn't noticed before lay behind him on the peeling floorboards. 'Yeah, anyway, bring home some beer, will you? And don't take long.'

The dirt from the verandah would ruin Pran's grey cotton pants but he was too exhausted to stay on his feet. The streets in this neighbourhood were desolate and confusing in their sameness. On his map the courts and crescents wound around each other like snakes. Spindly wilted gum trees stuck out from bald nature strips, and house after house had nothing but broken toys and rubbish in the yard. No shade anywhere. In some yards the carcasses of dry weeds stood higher than Pran's head.

About every third house his footsteps would detonate an explosion of barking. Mongrels, most of them, but occasionally a rottweiler or a pit bull would push its brutish head through a gate and stare at Pran as he passed. A few streets ago he had seen a weatherboard Church of Christ, surrounded by gravel and dumped cars. The windows of the church were boarded up.

Yet despite the dusty quiet of the hot streets and the empty yards, everyone was home. That morning in the office the team leader had said the area rated seventy per cent unemployment, so he told Pran and James not to turn up their noses like that. 'This is where the sales are. You

4

won't do any good in Toorak. They've got everything they need. This is where you'll make some money.'

The team leader had been right. Pran had overtaken his personal-best daily sales figure by eleven o'clock, and doubled it in the afternoon. He'd been about to take a short cut through this street and cross the reserve to his car when he saw the blonde on the verandah. She wore a faded yellow singlet and blue satin boxing shorts, and sat on an old stuffed armchair. Strapped to the stub of her leg under the left knee was a metal prosthesis with a running shoe fitted over a rubber foot. Her right foot was bare.

Pran knew he'd make a sale here.

It took a while for the cold tap to run cold water. Marly used to catch the warm water in a basin, then pour it later on the two-dollar punnet of pansies she'd planted in the square of dirt outside the back door, but they died so she didn't bother anymore. She waited with her hand in the stream of water, enjoying the sensation of the water cooling down. She thought about the pipes running underground, and wished there was some way they could use them to cool the whole house. On days like this, when the mercury rose above thirty, the flat roof sucked in the heat and it was five degrees hotter inside than outside, according to the thermometer Shaun kept on the kitchen wall.

'It's only out of the tap.' She handed the glass to the man, who was mopping his brow with a white handkerchief.

'Thank you very much.'

'You're not here about God, are you? Or Jesus? I'm not religious.'

'No, madam. I am Hindu. Our gods are many and we do not proselytise.'

In rehab, when she was learning to use her new metal leg after the accident, the man working with the other physio in the room had said he thought his disability was a message from the Lord Jesus. 'He made me this way and I don't dispute it,' he'd proclaimed, waving around his stumpy arm with its fused fingers. 'I see it as extra rungs on the ladder to heaven, given to me free and clear as compensation for this damn flipper and the bits that I haven't got.' The physio strapped a harness to the man's torso and helped him to ease into the contraption that took the place of his missing legs. 'I just hope,' the man said, 'that this fancy new equipment doesn't deduct from my extra allocation of grace.'

The Paki man drained the last of the water and placed the glass carefully beside the verandah post. Cable had finally stood up and shaken the loose dirt from his bristly brown coat. He wandered across the yard to sniff the feet of the new visitor.

'What kind of dog is this?' The man leaned backward, away from Cable – who, she had to admit, stank.

'It's a bitser. You know, bitser this and bitser that.'

The man tilted his head to the side. From this angle he was even more beautiful. Marly thought he should be a model or a TV star, not some loser walking around the suburbs trying to sell stuff.

'What is it you want to sell, anyway?'

'I tell you, madam, I am not here to sell you anything. I am here to give you something for nothing. I know it sounds unbelievable, but it is true.'

'Yeah, sure it is. And will you stop calling me madam? My name is Marly.'

'Pleased to meet you, Marly. My name is Pran.'

He held out his hand and she brushed her fingers against it, expecting to find the skin moist with sweat, but it was dry and cool.

He nodded at her leg. 'I am very sorry to see you have a disability. It must be hard to get out and about.'

'It's not so bad. When I put on jeans you hardly know it's there.' She thought again about the man whose flipper and missing limbs pushed him up the rungs of heaven. Her leg would hardly count for a single rung. When it first happened, she thought the men would run when they saw it, but she'd found the opposite. She used to say to her girlfriends that having half a leg had ended up being a bloke magnet, in a weird way. All of them falling over themselves to prove they were cool about it. 'Because it's discreet,' one of them had said. 'If you've got to have something wrong with you, it's good that it's discreet.' Marly knew what he meant, but it was more than that. Hep C was discreet. Having a bra stuffed with padding because of cancer was discreet. This was something else. And at that point it was better to stop thinking about it because it started to feel creepy.

'How long have you been in Australia?'

'Strange that you should ask. In fact, today is the anniversary of my arrival, seven years ago. I came as an undergraduate student at Monash University, then I completed an MBA. Now I am looking for employment in my field.'

'You must be pretty smart, then.' Marly's sister always talked about wanting to do an MBA. Marly was going to heap shit on her now. Get an MBA and you can walk the streets selling door to door.

'So Pran, let's cut the crap. What are you selling?' Marly collapsed back into the lounge chair at the other end of the verandah. It had been two years since the accident but she still leaned to her good side when she stood too long, and the aching would start in her hip and shoulder. 'I told you my husband was coming home soon, right? He's got a mate with him too.'

Sometimes she thought she and Shaun had a psychic bond. Like before, when she was playing with her phone wishing she had credit and then a few minutes later he'd called. Now he and Azza turned the corner into the street, the ute so polished and bright that its red gleam reflected off the fibro walls of the houses either side.

'See? Here he is.' In a movie she would leap off the verandah and run in slow motion toward the ute, her hair streaming behind, white dress fluttering in the breeze. But these days all she could do was stump around. The rubber foot connected with the ground at an odd angle, and she could feel it jar through her body with every step.

The boys pulled in to the yard and eased themselves up out of the ute that Shaun had lowered so far it almost dragged along the ground. They stood staring at Pran for a moment. Azza snickered. He turned his head so only Shaun and Marly could see his face and mouthed the word *Paki*.

'Shit,' Shaun said loudly. 'A fuckin' curry-muncher.'

'Good evening.' Pran stood and extended his hand, grateful that this would be his last sticky, grimy handshake of the day. The first thing he did when he got home each night was to take a long cool shower with antibacterial soap. Too bad if there was a water shortage. He needed to get clean after walking streets like these.

Neither of the men offered a hand in return. The tall one with the shaved head turned to the woman on the verandah.

'What's he selling?'

She shrugged. 'Did you bring the beer?'

'Here, gimme the slab, Azza. I'll put it in the fridge.'

Pran watched the bald man heft the slab into his muscular arms and cradle it like a baby as he leaped onto the verandah and opened the screen door with his foot. It slammed behind him. The other man lifted two large pizza boxes from the cab of the ute and walked up the steps past Pran, the thick smell of the pizza following him, and the dog drifting along behind, nose held high as if it was riding the aroma. At the door, the man paused. He balanced the pizza boxes on one bulky arm and with his free hand brushed his thick black hair back from his forehead.

'Why is it always Pakis knocking on the door? Don't they hire Australians anymore?'

Pran laughed. 'Please, take my job. I earn seven dollars an hour.' It was a lie. He was a natural salesman. He made a good living from these people. 'But actually, I am not Pakistani. I am from Delhi, the capital of India.'

'Right. That makes all the difference.' The man laughed and passed through the door, dog following, leaving the screen door jammed open against a buckled floorboard.

'Shut the frigging door, Azza! The flies get in.' The woman hauled herself out of the armchair and thumped along the verandah.

'Sorry,' she said to Pran, stepping into the house and pulling the screen door shut behind her.

He listened to the uneven thud of her walking down the hallway. He would have liked one more glass of water, although when he looked again at the glass it was dirty. Still, he lifted it, tilted it high and waited for the single drop from the bottom to roll the length of the glass and fall onto his parched tongue. He put the glass back on the boards and gazed down the street to where the reserve began. Only a ten-minute walk to his car. The reserve was a patch of bushland that seemed to have been forgotten by the council or whoever created it. Even from here, Pran could see that the wooden barrier at the entrance had been torn out and cars had been driven in. A mattress was propped against the fence of a house adjoining the reserve and further inside, under the trees, was the glint of broken glass.

'Thirsty, mate?' The bald man's voice came from behind the darkness of the screen door.

'Shaun, don't, please.' The woman's voice echoed down the hallway. 'Leave the guy alone.'

'Come on, mate, don't be shy. We'll shout you a beer.'

'You're very kind.' Pran used the verandah post to pull himself up. He was stiff from the long day of walking. 'I'm not a beer drinker, but another glass of water …'

'I think we can rustle that up for you.'

Pran gathered his clipboard and bag and walked into the house past the bald man, who held the door wide with his arm.

When the Indian stepped into the room and smiled at her, Marly's stomach flipped. He had been so serious before, an unsmiling manikin, but now that he had opened his face she wanted to touch his soft brown lips with her fingertips, run her tongue along his perfect white teeth. She felt the heat in her face and pushed herself up from the table.

'I'll find some ice,' she said. 'I think there's a tray in the fridge in the shed.'

By the time she got back with the ice cubes melting in the tray, Shaun and Azza were sitting at one end of the laminex table with the half-empty pizza boxes in front of them, while Pran perched on a chair in the opposite corner of the room near the stove.

'He doesn't eat meat,' Shaun said through a mouthful of pizza.

'But I am most grateful for you offering it to me.' Pran was holding his glass at chest height. When he raised it in a salute to the men, Marly saw that one of them had filled it with whisky. The Indian was so slim that half the amount would probably knock him out.

'Here, let me fix that up for you.' She emptied most of the whisky into another glass, then filled his glass to the brim with water and ice before handing it back. 'This should cool you down a bit.'

'You are very kind.' He lifted the glass to his lips and sipped at it.

Marly watched closely. The whisky was the cheapest you could buy. She couldn't drink it without drowning it in Coke. But the man's angelic face didn't flinch.

'I see you have a plasma television.' Pran nodded toward the screen, which was visible through the doorway into the lounge. It was a fifty-inch model Shaun had bought when they got the government bonus last year.

'Brilliant for watching the footy.' Azza directed his words to Marly, as if he couldn't bear to speak to the Indian. 'Right, mate?' He said this to Shaun.

'That's why I bought it.' Shaun reached for the pizza box and passed the second-last piece to Marly before taking the last one, rolling it into a tube and stuffing it whole into his mouth.

Marly took a bite and chewed on the salty, meaty, oily slice. She loved pizza. Sometimes eating was almost as good as sex, like now, with the capricciosa sitting warm in her belly and a mouthful of fizzy sweet beer to wash it down. That Indian guy didn't know what he was missing.

'They say that next year all the football will be on pay television.' Pran took another delicate sip of the whisky and water. This time Marly thought she saw his jaw clench as he swallowed.

'Got it.' Shaun pulled a roll of paper towels from the bench behind him. He tore off four sheets and passed the roll to Azza before wiping his mouth and hands and tossing the used towels at the bin in the corner. 'You're here to sell us Foxtel, right?'

'No, sir.'

'That other one, then. Optus, or Star, or whatever it is.'

'Sir, I am not here to sell you a single thing.'

'Fuck, he's really starting to piss me off now.' Azza spoke to the ceiling.

'Your name is Azza, I believe you said? Where are you from, sir?' Pran seemed unperturbed. He swivelled a little on his seat to face Azza.

'I'm from Thomastown, mate.' Azza had gone quite still.

'And your family? They are from Thomastown too?'

'They're from Lebanon. Not that it's any of your fucking business.'

Pran nodded and took another sip of the whisky.

'So come on, give us your spiel.' Shaun rocked back on his chair and rested his thonged feet on the edge of the kitchen table like he was getting ready to hear a story.

'I have no spiel. All I have for you is a free offer. No obligations, no payments, no commitments.'

'Go on.' Shaun was enjoying himself. Marly remembered the time he got the Mormons in and toyed with them for an hour and a half. She'd been drinking that night and so had he, and the evening was blurry – but the Mormons had never pressed charges, even though she'd found a piece of tooth in the glass on the floor the next morning, and it wasn't Shaun's and it wasn't hers.

'Do Hindus believe in God?' Marly interrupted. If she could break the chain, tonight might end differently.

'We have many gods, which are manifestations of a single reality. We believe in reincarnation, and in karma. What you choose to do in your life determines your destiny in this life and the next.'

'Sounds like that chick in the crystal shop.' Azza tipped back on his chair too, and swigged his beer.

'Take your feet off the table, boys. It's not nice.' Marly tapped her nails on the tabletop. The Indian's clean white shirt and his polished shoes were flickering like soft candles in the corner of the room.

Shaun and Azza were so surprised that they lifted their feet and dropped their chairs back to the floor.

'Jesus, Marl, where'd the manners suddenly come from?' Shaun reached across the table. He picked up a tube of toothpicks from the bench. He offered them around the table, but Azza and Marly shook their heads. The room was quiet as he rooted around the back of his mouth and brought out the toothpick to examine it. The tip was bright with blood, like a thin match.

'So.' Shaun rubbed the toothpick between his thumb and forefinger, twirling it up and down the length of his thumb pad. 'So, Pran, mate.'

'Yes, Shaun?'

Marly couldn't believe how relaxed he was. Either he was stupid or he had some secret weapon.

'Pran, I don't think we'll be taking your offer of a free set of steak knives.'

'I am not trying to offer you steak knives, Shaun.' Pran lifted his canvas bag and brought out a pamphlet. 'I am giving you free of charge six months of—'

'I said we don't want it, mate. The thing is—'

'Mr Pran, what did you mean by manifestations of a single reality?' Marly knew Shaun and Azza would be cursing her, but she had to make it stop. And maybe this calm little man had the secret. The secret of being happy, or of not always wanting to be someone else, somewhere else.

Pran wondered how the woman had ended up with these louts. 'You see, Marly, our scripture, the Bhagavad Gita, says that there is a single essence that underlies all existence. You might call it the soul. "The soul dwells in every living being, and in every part of every living being; it dwells in the hand and the foot, the skull and the mouth, the eye and the ear."' Pran watched Marly move her lips as he spoke, as if she was trying to make his words fit into ones she might understand. 'But for us in this world, it is only necessary to do one's duty.'

'You're giving me a headache, Pran.' Shaun finished his beer and lowered the bottle to the table. 'I think we're done here.'

'But I want to hear more. This is interesting.' Marly nodded at Pran and he saw the tension in her tight forehead. 'Come on, Shauny. Let him tell us a bit more.'

'Yeah, Shauny,' Azza whined in a mock falsetto, 'let's hear what the Paki has to say.' His voice dropped to its normal register. 'But you've gotta ask, if they've got it all worked out where he comes from, what's he doing here?'

'Come on.' Shaun leaped up from the table, his big body causing the room to tremble. 'We'll walk you to your car, mate.'

'I'm fine, thank you. It is very near.' Pran thought about the reserve and its bits of glass and discarded car parts. Outside, it was getting dark. The bush in the reserve would be dry and still and shadowy. He wasn't sure whether a path led straight through to the street where his car was sitting. Perhaps it would be wiser to take the long way around.

'Nope, I insist. Where is it?'

'Really, I don't want you to bother.' Perhaps these men thought they could attack him, take money from him. As if he would be stupid enough to carry money around a suburb like this. Pran eased his clipboard into his canvas bag and shook it until the clipboard had slid completely inside. 'Unless you feel like a walk. Company is always pleasant.'

'That's us, pleasant company. Right, Azza?'

'Right.' Azza stood and hitched up his jeans. 'Let's do it.'

Before he headed for the door, Pran turned and dipped his head to Marly. She was looking at him as if she felt sorry for him.

'What you are suffering in this world' – he waved his hand at Marly's prosthetic foot, but his eyes were trained on her face – 'will serve you in the next life.'

'Great, 'cause it's not doing her much fucking good in this one.' Shaun laughed as he positioned his big hand on the back of Pran's neck and guided him out of the kitchen.

Marly was waiting in the chair on the front verandah when the boys walked back through the hole in the fence. Neither of them looked at her. As she followed them into the house, a creased sheet of paper eased out of Shaun's back pocket and fluttered to the floor. He didn't notice until Marly had stooped to pick it up, then he turned and tried to snatch it from her. She stared at the printed sheet with Shaun's scrawled signature at the bottom. 'What's this?'

Shaun tried again to nab the paper from her fingers but Marly held on.

'A minimum of two thousand dollars over twenty-four months – are you fucking kidding? How did he get you to sign this?' As she threw the paper onto the kitchen table, she noticed Azza thrust his hands in his pockets, but not before she had caught sight of the rusty brown stain on his palm.

'Oh, no. What did you do to him?' She pictured Pran's melty eyes swimming with tears of pain, his soft mouth squeezed into a grimace. 'Where is he?' If they'd hurt that beautiful man she was going to kill them.

'He's all right, okay? I lost it for a minute, tapped him on the nose.' Azza pulled his hand from his pocket, spat on it and rubbed it against his jeans until the stain was off his skin.

'That's blood.'

'He's all right. We said we were sorry. He drove away in his fucking Honda coupe. Now shut up.' Shaun slammed his fist on the table. The dog bolted out through the back door.

Marly stood uncertainly in the doorway. Shaun was glaring at her, daring her to say a single word. She'd never find out how the Indian had got him to sign the contract.

'I'm going out front.' She took a beer from the fridge and stumped down the hallway to the verandah on her graceless steel leg. The streetlights were on. She could see the shadows of trees in the reserve. On the other side, somewhere, was Pran, flying along the freeway in his Honda coupe with two thousand dollars of their money. Money they didn't even have yet. Two years of their lives signed away. Everything had turned upside down. She tried to remember what he had said about the essence. Something about hands and feet. Or skulls and ears. Or something.

Procession

When they first stood up and walked on their hind legs we paid money to see them.

I took my five-year-old. She laughed and ran up to one of the dogs, who stood upright beside a bucket where we were supposed to drop our tickets. Sienna was the same height as the Beagle. He laid a paw on her shoulder. His sinewy tongue curled for a moment around the lobe of her ear and she giggled, kissing the dog's wet black nose before she ran back to me. I pulled a wipe from my bag to clean her face as she chattered.

'His name is Oscar but he doesn't like it.' She grinned her toothy grin at me as I screwed up the wipe and threw it in the bin. 'A human gave him the name.'

'A person, you mean. Like me or Daddy or your teacher.'

'Yes, a person.'

In the ring, the dogs performed tricks people had taught them in the old circus. An Airedale played the ringmaster. He strutted across the sandy floor with a whistle clenched between his teeth, gesturing with his front paws to direct the performers around the stage. A Toy Poodle rode the shoulders of a loping Great Dane. Ten Border Collies formed a precarious pyramid, tumbled barking to the ground, bounced up and paraded around the ring for our applause.

The chests of the bitches were fluffy, but below the ribs the fur thinned and soft skin showed through, mottled black and white in the same pattern as their coats. They looked strangely vulnerable beside the parading dogs. When dogs walk on their hind legs, they display their cock and balls like ostentatious jewellery. The castrated dogs walked differently from the ones who were still entire. With their small empty sacs tucked up close to their bodies and their cocks thrust far forward they walked as if they were about to lose their balance. But they never did.

'I want to go again tomorrow,' Sienna demanded.

'No. Tomorrow is your swimming lesson, remember?'

'I don't care. I want to see them again.'

On the walk home we passed a cobblestoned lane, shadowy in the late dusk, stinking of city garbage. Two mixed-breed dogs stood with their shoulders against the south wall of the lane. In the past I would have called them mongrels. They faced each other and made throaty grunts, their tails snapping against the brickwork.

I asked Sienna what they were saying. Only children and a very few adults could understand the dogs' guttural conversations punctuated with sharp barks and whines. Academics were studying recordings of them talking but their progress was slow. It was easier to ask a child what was going on.

'They're having a talk,' she said. She licked ice-cream off her hand where it had dripped.

'I can see that. A talk about what?'

Sienna took another long lick of her chocolate ice-cream before looking away from me and answering, 'I couldn't hear very well.'

I think that was the first wilful lie she told me.

Not all the dogs developed at the same rate. Our dog, Pugsley, was at home behaving like the dog we'd always known, shitting all over the yard, barking at shadows, goofing around with Sienna and her father, Adrian, until very late in the piece.

I suppose, now I think about it, that it was the clown dogs who were the last to turn. Pugs, Basset Hounds, Boxers. The working dogs led the change. The first dog I saw standing up was a Blue Heeler bitch. She watched me walk past, my mouth open in amazement, and she coughed as I was about to turn the corner. When I swung to face her she wagged her tail slowly, languorously, looking me straight in the eye. That was the moment I knew everything had changed. Not the hind-leg walking but a dog gazing at me as if we were equals.

Once everything settled down we went back to shopping at the supermarket, but in the early weeks of fear that the dogs might attack, shops were closed and people were guarding their goods and property. I went to the cupboard and found tiny jars of anchovies, truffle-infused olive oil, the hand-ground dukkah Adrian liked to bring home from his work trips to Egypt. Sensible people went to their cupboards and found flour, sugar, tins of baked beans and soup.

I asked my neighbour if I could swap a packet of roasted almonds for a piece of fresh fruit for Sienna. She went inside to get an apple but her husband came out instead, red-faced and stinking of beer.

'I haven't forgotten the fucking car, you bitch,' he said.

I stepped back, stomach whirling in fear.

'Didn't the insurance company pay you?' I said, my voice squeaky. I wasn't sure whether to stay or run. 'I did the paperwork. I sent it in ages ago.' I had rolled into the back of their car in the street – dented the bumper bar and cracked a rear light.

He lurched forward as if he would fall on his face, then grabbed the architrave and pulled himself upright.

'We never had a dog. It's cunts like you who brought this on,' he said, and slammed the door.

I stood there shaking. Their seven-year-old son pulled aside the lounge room curtain and stared out at me, his pale fat face void of expression. He looked like he'd never eaten a piece of fruit in his life.

It's been eight years, but I still remember the circus and our wide-eyed admiration of those first few dogs. I remember the fear and panic that grew as more dogs changed. People with guns, behaving like savages. I remember the day the government declared the dogs protected against the vigilantes. The bill of rights, the opening of the compounds.

What I can't place is the exact moment last year when I realised Sienna had joined the Dogteens. She turned into a stranger while we worried about installing a new security system.

Last night she came home late, as usual, and flung herself on the couch in front of the television.

'Senn, please don't wear the furs on the furniture,' I said. 'Have you had dinner? How was school? Where have you been?'

She sat up, peeled off the stitched-together fur-scrap poncho, and tossed it on the floor beside the couch. Underneath she was wearing a T-shirt with a Chihuahua transfer and a pair of cut-off jeans. I noticed a bruise on her throat near the collarbone.

'Take the fur outside and leave it on the verandah. It's disgusting.'

'In a minute,' she said. I watched the bruise disappear and reappear as she rubbed it with her fingers.

'Have you hurt yourself? Let me take a look.'

'Leave me alone.'

'Come on, sweetheart, let me have a look. A dog didn't bite you, did it?'

I saw it on a current affairs show last week. One of the Dogteens who'd broken away was interviewed. Her profile was in darkness, her voice disguised by technology and sounding uncannily like the gruff tones of a dog. She said the dogs in the inner compound nip the Dogteens to break their skin and infect them with a virus that turns their fingernails into claws and sharpens their hearing and sense of smell. Those teenagers, the ones who have been bitten, are the ones who never come home. I don't know why I kept watching. I never watch those stupid shows.

'Of course not. They'd never bite us.' Sienna's hand crept up to her throat and massaged the purple mark.

'Here,' I said, picking the stinking furs off the floor and stretching out my hand to help her off the couch, 'I'll put some antiseptic on it. Please, darling.'

'Fuck off,' she said. As she turned her head away to watch the TV I thought I heard a sound, a rumble from deep in her chest.

My heart started to beat faster. 'Did you growl at me?'

She rolled her eyes and snuggled deeper into the rug on the couch. I could feel the greasy furs leaving their stink on my hands as I hurried to the verandah to hang them on the outside hook. The schools do the same thing – they have a shed at the end of the schoolyard where the Dogteens can hang their furs. I've tried washing them but Sienna will only come home with a different mangy collection of pelts. She wants to smell. Like her Dogteen friends she hates to be reminded she's human.

This morning we were all up early. Outside, the sky was an eerie watermelon colour. Clouds were gathering to the north, furling over the horizon in fat greys and purples. Adrian, home all weekend for a change, pushed eggs around the frypan and I buttered toast while Sienna stood on the verandah, her head high, sniffing the wind.

'I'll have bacon,' she called in through the window.

'You ate it all yesterday.' Adrian shut the window and turned to me. 'Or maybe she rubbed it over herself. Soon she'll stink so badly I won't be able to stand in the same room as her. What happened to our daughter? Can't you get her to take a shower?'

'Can't you?' The words burst out of me. I wanted to suck them back in. I didn't want a fight. I hate to fight.

I didn't dare tell him about the turd, or the cat's tail with scraps of pink flesh still hanging from it, or the rutting. She's a teenager, I told myself the night I heard her grunting and barking in the backyard with the boy who looks like a dingo, all pale bristly hair and pointy face. She's had her implant so she won't get pregnant. But the turd. The little exclamation mark of dried-up poo I found nestled behind her bedroom door. How could I explain that?

'At least she's here for breakfast. She'll turn out all right, you'll see. You know most of them grow out of it.' I felt my face wrinkle into an appeasing smile.

'That's if we still want her.'

'Thanks a lot, Dad.' Sienna had slunk inside and was crouched on her haunches in the corner of the room, beside the door to the lounge.

'You know I don't mean it.' He was smiling at her. He reached down to tousle her hair but she cringed further into the corner.

'Darling, come and sit at the table,' I said. 'I'll cook you sausages.'

She sneezed and scratched behind her ear. The soft curls of her strawberry blonde hair bounced as she scratched. Her foot thumped the floor. I could hear the packs of Dogteens gathering out in the streets, whooping and baying and shrieking as they did every weekend on their way to the local compound.

'Forget it.' She rose to her feet in a fluid movement that took her out the back door in three long paces. 'I'll see you later. I'm in the traces today.'

As soon as she'd gone I sat down heavily on the kitchen chair.

'She's been bitten,' I said to Adrian. 'Did you see her neck? And she's going to be hauling that dog!'

'She's been bitten, all right. Some boy giving her a love bite.'

'No, no. I think it's one of those dog bites where they pass on the virus.'

Adrian held his fork mid-air, balancing a triangle of toast topped with a wobbly pyramid of scrambled egg. For a moment he did nothing, then he guided the food to his mouth and chewed slowly and swallowed.

'I want to take her to the doctor.' I heard the crack in my voice.

He put down his cutlery, edged his chair close to mine, and hugged me. I hadn't noticed that my husband had got plump like me until then, when his belly moulded over my left arm. His double chin rested on my shoulder. His arms could barely encircle my torso. We were two Humpty dolls. I began to laugh. He held me tighter. He thought I was crying.

'That TV show is complete rubbish. You know that,' he murmured into my hair.

'I know,' I said, between giggles.

He let go. I took his hand in mine, pressed his palm against my cheek. My giggles had subsided. A strange despair crept over me.

'How did we get so old?'

Every Sunday afternoon the leader of the dogs, the pack-master, is towed on a float around the centre of town by thirteen Dogteens in harness. The remaining Dogteens, perhaps three or four hundred in this city, run alongside the float with the dog pack, laughing and shouting in that guttural canine tongue few adults have ever mastered, banging on drums and blowing whistles and doing cartwheels and funny dances.

Adrian and I take the tram into town, and we settle at a cafe's outdoor table. The young woman serving us, perhaps in her early twenties, is wearing a pair of clip-on dog ears. A fake fur tail hangs from the seat of her jeans. The cafe is called Dogster.

'Here for the parade?' she asks as she takes our orders.

The city mutters in an expectant, festive conversation. There is an occasional rumble of distant thunder and the light is a yellowy purple. Whiffs of stale oil and rotten garbage and the leftover rank smell of Saturday night in the city swirl through the air.

'If we had a normal daughter, this would be a netball final or a school concert. You'd better be right about her growing out of it soon.' Adrian blows on his coffee and takes a hesitant sip.

He's not ready for this. He spends too much time away, a life behind glass in cars and planes and offices. He's only just realised his daughter stinks. She's not simply our daughter anymore. She's a Dogteen. An independent wild thing who will do whatever she wants.

I can hear the procession coming down the next street. The drums and tambourines bang out unevenly and tin whistles are playing tunes, but most of all it's the barking and growling and yapping that echoes off the walls of the tall city buildings. Some comes from the dogs, some is recognisably human.

Sunday shoppers are heaving their bags through the streets and a few people line the footpath, waiting for the parade to pass. In the electronics shop next to the cafe, I can see a telecast of the float coming down Collins Street. The packmaster, a bizarre red-dreadlocked cross between a Hungarian Puli and a Kelpie, sits on a massive purple satin cushion on the float, flanked on each side by identical Pekingese trotting along the road like an undulating carpet. This week they're escorting a float in the shape of a giant bone. That's what we never expected – the sense of humour, the practical jokes, the sheer joy of life the dogs bring to every event. That's how they seduce our children.

The second they round the corner, tears spring to my eyes. I don't know whether I'm proud or ashamed. Sienna is the lead child in the harness. The chosen one. Leather straps criss-cross her chest, wrinkling the worn fabric of her shirt and carving a crevasse between her bud breasts. The harness and the float are strung with bells and medallions, ribbons and tattered pieces of coloured cloth.

As she strains to pull the float, her jaw clenches and the ropes of muscle vibrate in her throat. I want to run over and strip her out of that harness, take her home, wash her in a hip bath. I'd dress her in a clean pair of flannelette pyjamas and feed her mashed vegetables and read to her from a girls' adventure book as she drifted off to sleep in the soft light of her bedroom.

Sienna lifts her arms, and the children in the harness rear back and finally stop. The packmaster stands. There's an exchange between him and Sienna, yelping and barking, a growl. The packmaster circles three times and curls up on the cushion while Sienna talks to the children in harness behind her. As we're waiting to find out what this means, a Pug leaves the procession, trots across the road to me and sits at my feet, grinning up at me with its wrinkled face.

'Pugsley?' I don't know what to do. They don't like to be petted anymore.

Pugsley rises to his feet, backs off and yaps three times at us before turning and haring into the group of dogs, his squat hindquarters pumping like pneumatic cushions.

'Did you see that?' I place my hand on Adrian's arm, but he's staring at Sienna.

The procession has quietened down. Sienna gazes straight at me and nods. After I have smiled and waved she tilts her head back, exposing her bony white throat, and begins a howl, a low moan that rises fast into an aria of leaping and bones and shitting and wild scents and twitching dreams all braiding into a brutal joyous crescendo of freedom. When she finishes, the whole city is silent. She turns her head to us again. The bells on her harness tinkle. Below her furs and checked cotton shorts, the long tense muscles of her thighs tremble. Adrian is watching with his mouth open.

The packmaster barks once, and Sienna and the other children in the traces leap forward, wrenching against the leather like I remember Pugsley doing years ago on his first walk outside the yard.

A child behind Sienna trips and claws at Sienna's furs to steady herself. Sienna turns and snarls. Her braces glint like metal jewellery. A light rain is starting to drift across the street.

'I hope she's not wearing those trainers with the hole,' I say. 'I told her to throw them out.'

'Jesus Christ.'

I look where he is looking. A young girl at the rear of the parade is squatting. A shiny stream of piss winds its way along the black road in front of her. She leaps up, her skirt falls against her thighs, and she races to her spot behind the float, fur jacket bouncing against her torso in time with her jumps and pirouettes. Three boys press into the spot where she has pissed and lean in to sniff. One of them barks, the other two fall back, and he unzips his fly and covers her puddle with his own frothy yellow stream.

Adrian has knocked over his coffee cup with his elbow and the spill is creeping across the table. I use a napkin to dam the flow. The drummers ramp up the beat and the procession moves on.

When our waitress brings a sponge to the table she has to ask Adrian to lift his elbow. He turns and stares at her as though he can't understand a single word she has said.

'Sorry, it's all a bit much for him.' I tug a few more napkins from the dispenser and press them against Adrian's damp jacket sleeve as the waitress pulls a dishcloth from her apron pocket.

'I know.' She rubs the table briskly and sets the salt and pepper shakers in their basket. 'I mean, they're kind of cute in a way, I suppose. But filthy. And weird, you know.'

Her words break through Adrian's catatonic stare. He frowns, as if to himself. I wait with my hands clenched around the damp napkins, hoping that this is the moment I have been waiting for all these years. *Claim her*, I am urging him silently. *Claim your daughter.*

31

The tail end of the procession is dancing away from us. Adrian sighs. He turns and gives me a disappointed look, as if it's all my fault.

The City Circle

I live in a suburb where no politician lives and therefore the trams run infrequently, often late and without proper brakes. Two, three times a month, when the driver applies a little pressure to the pedal, we are all sent hurtling to the front of the tram like atoms in a particle accelerator, ready to smash against a plate and separate into our constituent parts. Last month, in a particularly violent trajectory toward the wall, two of us tumbled to the floor. The woman next to me apologised in accented English for falling. A man in a smart suit rushed to her aid.

'Are you all right?' he whispered. She nodded.

'And you?' the man said to me.

'I'm fine, thanks,' I said.

The man handed a business card to the woman, who was looking thin and alarmed. He handed another to me, who, on the other hand, was looking large and robust, with only my clothes and my composure askew. I knelt, then stood, shrugging my suit jacket and throttling my tie back into position.

I read the business card as the lawyer pressed the woman.

'Are you on your way to work? Are you a permanent resident? Do you understand what I'm saying?'

The tram driver eased the vehicle to a halt at the tram stop. He came down to help the woman. When he asked if she was able to get up, the lawyer thrust out his arm to prevent the tram driver from touching her.

'For God's sake,' he said to the driver, 'call an ambulance.'

'No,' the woman said. 'I okay. I have to go work now. Please.'

'You don't have to go to work. Everything is going to be all right. The ambulance is coming.'

I knew this scenario from American cop shows. Layers of mystery would unfold from this woman's unexceptional tumble on a tram. Forty-two television minutes later, drug busts would ensue, or a paedophile ring would be smashed and the cleric would hang himself.

'No ambulance,' the woman said. She used the lawyer's arm to haul herself up, straightened her dress, and then waved him away. End of crime-show plot.

'Folks, I'm going to have to report a brake fault,' the driver called out. 'Might take a few minutes for the engineers to get back to me.'

Up the other end of the tram another cluster of atoms was forming, atoms who were going to be late for work and who couldn't decide who to blame – the tram driver, the lawyer, me, the woman who'd fallen to the floor, the transport corporation, the government. So they got off the tram. I followed. We trooped down the road to the next intersection, where the tracks of an alternative route snaked in twin wires toward town.

Ten minutes later we set off on another tram, padded shoulder jammed against breast pocket. My arm pressed against the woman beside me. The back of my arm was gently riding her ribs, up and down, like I was playing a musical instrument with frets every few centimetres. One fret higher and my elbow would meet her breast. I couldn't help imagining its curved bell shape moulding against my arm. I glanced surreptitiously at her face and saw that she was gaunt and beautiful and so heavily made up it was impossible to tell what colour her real skin might be. Her lips were a startling purple.

Compared to the woman who had fallen, I was tall, but standing next to this commuter I was medium-sized. A medium-sized commuter on my way to a medium-sized job in a medium-sized city that I know too well.

I thought about how if I stayed in this city long enough I would run into the long angular woman at a party. I would spend some time wondering how I knew her face. She might do the same. We'd smile at each other in an I-know-you-from-somewhere kind of way and we might banter with a few jokes and offer to get another drink and move on to a few words about how we happened to know the person who was hosting the party and then we would inch a little closer, laugh a little louder, touch a little more often until it was late enough for us to slip away. Or we might each go off and find someone else to talk to, or we might stand together uncomfortably for a while and then separately decide we were tired after a week of work and it was time to go home. But we wouldn't take a tram. She would call a taxi or hail one on the main street near the party, and I would walk on, pretending I was a big man, not afraid of the dark and the desperate drug addicts lurking inside shadows, but further down the road I'd hail a different taxi, one driven by a man from Somalia who would ask whether I knew the capital of Somalia and when I answered correctly wouldn't have anything else to say.

Tonight, with a storm thrumming on the window of the cafe and commuters bowing into the rain as they hurry along the street, another tram story begins – with someone my friend knows. Sometimes, after work, I meet my friend who works in a government department writing policy on the punctuality and frequency of public transport, and we drink white wine and eat bowls of hot chips and talk. When we first sat down, the story she had told me was this: a man had begun to act strangely in her office. He wore gaudy ties to important meetings.

'Great wide lurid things with smiley faces and ducks and fluorescent stop signs.' My friend shook her head.

I said I wished someone wore ties that interesting to meetings I attended.

'You don't understand,' she said. 'It's inappropriate. And he wears brown shoes with black suits, and he has greasy hair.'

When she mentioned the man's greasy hair, I wondered how long it was since I had washed my own. Before I could stop it, my hand had reached up to my head.

'Your hair's looking good,' she said, seeing me tentatively fingering strands, checking the grease factor. 'Have you had it trimmed?'

I remembered a man with greasy hair on my tram the other week. Strings of greasy hair. Greasy hair with a rancid smell, greasy hair with months of body oil and polluted rain and the fatty residue of meals brushed from the fingers – unintentionally of course – and thick flakes of dandruff embedded near the scalp. He was standing beside me and the stench was overwhelming. I moved away. After a few minutes all the other passengers had drifted away too and he stood in a vacant space, a tiny chapel on the tram. He was praying, loudly.

'Jesus Christ, Jesus fucking Christ. Jesus, Jesus.'

The space in his tram chapel expanded. He wasn't holding on to the handgrip and as the tram swayed and sashayed along the tracks he teetered backward and forward, the whole chapel moving as the other passengers edged away to avoid him like a raggedy chorus line. I realised I had seen him several times before on this line. Another of my intimate strangers on the tram.

'Have you got a fucking ticket?' he shouted. He took a step in my direction and I stepped back, onto the foot of someone behind me. She yelped. I apologised. Again. How often have I fallen, stumbled, tripped while on the tram?

How many times have I have crashed into people, struck them accidentally with my flailing hand or pushed my briefcase against them as I juddered forward, propelled by the motion of the tram? How often have I cracked a shin against the sharp corner of a seat, jarred my elbow on the ticket machine, been speared by the tip of another passenger's umbrella? How many passengers falling in what seems like slow motion have reached out and grabbed items of my clothing – sleeves, jackets, scarves – to break their fall? I have been dragged down and I have scrabbled on the floor. How much of my life have I spent struggling to get up?

The greasy-haired man was pointing at me as these questions crowded my head. I may have been muttering, or at least my lips may have been moving. The tram crowd edged away from me too. Greasy man and I were two magnetic poles and the commuters iron shavings being repelled by both.

At the next stop, greasy man turned his head when the doors opened. Three people hurried off under his gaze, shoulders hunched, their feet taking anxious baby steps. He looked at me once more with loathing.

'I am the great inspector,' he roared, and hurled himself off the tram just as the door was sliding shut.

The iron shavings rotated when he was gone. I was the only repellent left. Their bodies rotated away from me and I was left in my own lonely chapel on the tram. At least I still have a job, I thought. I might be mad, but I still have a job.

In the cafe with my friend, I dropped my hand from my hair and tried to focus on the conversation.

'I think he's losing it,' she repeated about her colleague with the lurid ties.

'Perhaps he's having a style makeover?'

'I don't think it's funny,' my friend answered crossly. 'So like I said, we're at this meeting …'

She kept talking while I pondered how linear her thinking had become since she started writing policy. This is why older, more experienced public servants should be given charge of policies that determine movement in the lives of the general public – they have had time for proper thinking patterns to form, time to appreciate and enjoy a vast range of humanity. They understand the cyclical nature of things. Older public servants would at least consider the possibility that a lurid tie may or may not be related to a simple need for understanding, and that it is wise not to make judgments without hearing the full case.

'Then he said he thought I had failed to appreciate the gravity of the situation.' My friend's mouth was open. She spread her hands and dropped her jaw and shook her head, begging me with the gesture to express my own astonishment.

'Huh,' I said, not too worried that I had missed the actual cause of the astonishment. Like a reliable service, the next one would be along soon.

'And then,' she went on, 'when I went to my head of department to—'

'This guy, tie guy, he writes policy too?' I interrupted.

'Yeah, forest management.'

'And he's how old?'

'Fifty, maybe sixty. He used to be brilliant at policy. Everyone hated what he did – the greenies, the logging industry. He always got it right.'

I imitated her gesture of astonishment back at her. The open palms, the hanging jaw, the wide eyes.

'Well,' she said defensively, 'if one of the groups loves the policy, everyone will think you've been lobbied.'

Lobbied – such a strange word. I thought of being hall-wayed or verandahed. Porched. My friend whose policy fails to ensure regular safe trams on my route continues with her story as I tick off more words. Porticoed. Entranced. There, I knew I would find a proper word. The man may have been entranced. I realise I am muttering the words aloud and my friend is staring at me. And you can see that now I'm telling you this story in present tense as if it's happening at this moment, even though I was using the past tense before, and before that I was in the present. Maybe this is happening now, or maybe the actions are completed. Or I could be imagining it all. Forward motion is rarely what it seems. We spend half our lives in the future while still thinking about the past and vice versa, in an endless loop of longing and regret.

'I just thought I'd talk to you about him,' she continues, still staring. 'Because you have, you know, experience with these … with … things.'

'Being mad?'

'Don't be stupid, you know what I mean. You've had a nervous breakdown, you know the signs, don't you? Are they, like, what's happening to this guy?'

I want to reach out with my hands in the most exaggerated motion I can manage in order to imitate her previous gesture of astonishment. And I want to snarl or bark or spit in her coffee or do something equally disturbing. But I am a responsible man in a responsible position. I don't do things like that.

So I lean back and say to her, 'Everyone has a nervous breakdown. Sometimes they're mild and hardly noticeable. Sometimes they're catastrophic. Eventually, we all go under. Every time I get on a tram I see someone heading for a breakdown. We're like machines, we can't just keep going on. We break down, then we get repaired and back on the tracks. Even you – one day you'll have one, even if you don't realise it yourself.'

I can see she's trying not to smirk with disbelief at the idea of being shunted off to the depot for an overhaul. And maybe I am being too smug. Maybe my policymaker friend won't break down at all. What would I know? All I can really be sure of is that everything would be more straightforward if I could spend my days riding the City Circle tram, the old W-class clanker that trundles tourists around town for free, around and around, with a conductor on board whose only job is to help.

'Did you write the policy on the City Circle trams?'

I ask my friend. She pauses, startled by the change of subject.

'That's the Tourist Authority,' she says. 'Not Infrastructure. I work in Infrastructure.'

She starts gathering her bag and coat. 'Got to get back to the grind,' she says, smiling. 'Briefing due tomorrow. Big night on the computer at home.'

'Yes, I think your forest man is heading for a breakdown,' I say.

Once more she does the astonishment gesture, but this time her head-waggle has a new knowingness about it.

'I knew it,' she says. 'No really, I knew it.'

She gets up and goes, paying for us both on the way out to the street, where the storm has passed and the wet black footpaths are softly steaming.

I often call the City Circle tram to mind, the gentle pace of it, the tourists hopping on and off. I'd like to pass the carefree image of the City Circle on to the greasy-haired man, or even to tie man, who might have already boarded the wrong tram. He probably feels like he's going places, he's got speed and modern technology on his side. At the same time he might be looking at the floor, starting to realise that it's a new kind of floor in a new kind of tram, flat and slippery and deceptive. In this city, you feel like you're riding high and easy, but there's a suddenness about things that always surprises you. Up the front, the driver is about to apply a little pressure to the brakes.

My friend blows me a kiss and walks off to her carpark.
I want to call after her. I want to tell her about the future.

You hit the wall, you disintegrate, you put yourself back together again.

No lawyer in the world can help you with that.

Stingers

We stood by the side of the Bruce Highway, highway number one, our packs on the gravel and our toes on the tarmac as if some contact with the road surface would give us the power to make trucks stop. The sun flared in the sky, a mirage shimmered halfway along the ribbon of grey stretching north, a swarm of bugs buzzed from inside the head-high feathery crops beside the road.

'Put out your thumb,' Josie said.

'You put yours out. You told me you're a champion hitcher.'

Josie cocked her hip at the oncoming car. She thrust out her hand with her thumb pointing skyward. It looked like something she'd learned from a movie. She had these gestures, these stances, phrases and winks that she tossed off like an actress. I'd longed for her careless grace all my life.

'Have you ever hitched before?' I asked. I'd forgotten a sun hat, and the top of my head was scorching. The word *scared* formed a swift surprising tension in my mind before evaporating like the wavy mirage up the road when trucks bored through it.

'No.'

The taxi from the airport had dropped us here on the side of the highway.

'It's unbeatable irony, Josie. We took a taxi here to start hitchhiking.' I poked through the bag of animal-shaped sweets in my shorts pocket until I found a coiled snake and popped it into my mouth. Josie had handed me the packet when I emerged from the aerobridge that morning. 'An introduction to the tropics and all its creepy critters,' she'd said. She was as thin as a snake herself, and dry, and somehow different from when I'd last seen her.

'Shut up and look sexy.'

We felt the road grinding under our soles as four cars and a truck roared past in a hail of grit and dust.

'Pull your top down a bit,' Josie said. 'Show us some of that famous cleavage.'

'I haven't got cleavage. I'm an A-cup.'

'God, I have to do everything.' Josie wiggled her torso and pushed and pulled at the bra under her purple singlet until a wrinkle of cleavage appeared.

'Push your biceps into your boobs. It'll make them look bigger.' I'd practised that plenty of times myself in the bathroom when I was a teenager, leaning forward, arms crushed to my sides, pouting and slitting my eyes, making love to my own reflection in the hope that one day I could fool some boy into believing I knew what I was doing.

'Why don't we just strip?'

'Why don't we strip and run out onto the road screaming?'

'Why don't you strip and lie down on the bitumen and I'll flag someone down like you're injured.'

We decided to walk back to town, stay the night and take the bus the next day. The next afternoon when the bus rolled up we congratulated ourselves on our wise decision, but I was aware that the bus was too tall for its width, like an over-decorated cake that could easily topple over. The inside of the bus smelled like people had been living in there. Down the side of my seat I found a used tissue and a ticket stub for the Reading Cinemas in Townsville.

'Yuck. Don't touch that,' Josie said. She batted at my hand with her pen until I dropped the tissue. 'That person might have had TB.'

An old man hacking away in the back of the bus sounded like he did have TB. The driver put Johnny Cash on the sound system. Josie was scribbling into a notebook.

'J & M's Travel Diary, Day One. We are losers and couldn't hitch a ride even when we showed our cleavage,' Josie read out.

Why am I here? I wondered.

At seven in the evening the bus spilled us into the dark wet air of Cairns. The driver hauled our packs from the belly of the bus. As the other passengers drifted away or opened up maps and started peering at street signs, Josie and I punched each other in the arm to wake ourselves up.

Around us were palm trees and assorted tropical plants breathing out steam. After we had changed our clothes in the nearest cafe toilet, we sat outdoors on plastic chairs in yellow light, inhaling the exhaust fumes and briny air.

'There are no pancakes on this menu,' Josie said to the waiter, a beanpole fired up with some kind of health mania, who bounced on the balls of his feet with his pen poised. 'I can't tell you how disappointing this is.'

'We could make you up a cinnamon buckwheat hotcake. It's pretty tasty and filling.'

Josie turned to me, her bare white thighs squeaking on the plastic chair. 'I want to go home.'

'She'll have the hotcake,' I said in my usual straight-guy role, 'and I'll have a mango smoothie.'

Josie already had her pen and diary out. I peered over her shoulder while she scratched away.

J & M's Travel Diary, Day Two. Cairns smells like a muck of sea, rotten fruit and dried cum. The people here have not yet discovered pancakes.

'What's with the diary? You're a writer now?'

'Yep. I grew tired of my free and easy retail-assistant life.'

Inside the hostel was a lounge filled with lounging backpackers wearing singlets, shorts and thongs.

'We brought the wrong uniform,' Josie said.

I couldn't see what she meant. Both Josie and I were wearing singlets, shorts and thongs.

Josie sighed. 'I wanted to find a different crowd. These people look like the ones we left at home.'

'No they don't. They look like exciting overseas travellers. They look like carefree young men and women looking for adventure.'

'Citizens of the globe. Happy wayfarers. Pioneers.'

'Or gap-year kids.'

'It's true. They're middle-class gap-year layabouts. I think we're too old for this. Twenty-six is ancient.'

'We should be in motels with fenced swimming pools.'

'A guide with a flag.'

'Hourly rest stops and emergency wheelchairs.'

'Have you got photo ID?' the girl behind the counter asked. 'I need to make copies.' She sounded resigned like the receptionist at the dentist, dealing with clients who have arrived miserable. I had thought that everyone in the tropics would be welcoming and have sweet breath. They would exude pineapple fragrance and optimism.

'People in the tropics should be happy,' I whispered to Josie as the girl hunched over the grey copy machine and stabbed buttons.

'I'm sure they are. This is an act to discourage us from staying. They want it all to themselves,' she whispered back.

The area around the counter was decked out with postcards pinned to a corkboard leaning against the wall, posters for Great Barrier Reef cruises and rainforest tours, ads for part-time salespeople and charity collectors, lost earrings and necklaces hanging on screw-in hooks, and a rubber marlin head looming over it all. Counter girl was filling in another form.

Josie reached up to touch the marlin's spike. 'I don't know how you talked me into this, Merryn.'

'I didn't,' I said. 'You sent me a ticket to fly to Townsville. You said we'd hitch up to Cape Trib and have a ball. You said this was the trip of a lifetime.'

'You're right. Let's have a shower and lather up with bug spray. The good folk of Cairns await us.'

At the pub, tables were clotted with backpackers conducting their travel conversations over jugs of beer and the crushed remains of silver chip packets. They wore singlets, shorts and thongs, and an array of fading tattoos.

'Tell me again, why are we here?' Josie asked.

The banter, our old clubby banter, was wrong, out of place. I didn't know how to stop it. I took a mouthful of the yeasty cold beer and held it while it fizzed on my tongue. On the big TV screen in the corner I could see pictures of Melbourne. Something must have happened. After the opening shot of the skyline there was an image of a police car and a reporter sticking a microphone into the face of a spiky-haired kid who couldn't hide his excitement at being on television. In between answering the reporter's questions he kept looking around as if he was waiting for someone to applaud.

'Let's go somewhere the locals go,' I said. 'I hate back-packers.'

Josie was still looking at the TV. 'That's Hoppers Crossing. I used to live in a street near that street.'

'Come off it. That could be any street. All you can see is a few weatherboard houses and a dumb kid talking to a reporter.'

'No, really. I walked along that street every day when I worked at the sandwich shop.'

'You did not work in a sandwich shop.'

'Did so. For a month in school holidays.'

'You would make shit sandwiches. You can't even slice cheese without the block falling apart.'

'I did make shit sandwiches. No one cared. They ate their shit sandwiches and enjoyed them.'

'Came back for more.'

'Daily. Sometimes they bought two shit sandwiches.' Josie stood, drained her beer, picked up her bag. 'Let's find that local joint. Meet some locals. If they're lucky I'll consider making them a shit sandwich.'

What's wrong? I wanted to ask her. *Why are we doing this stupid talk when you've flown me up here because something is terribly, awfully wrong?* But I couldn't ask. She had that power over people, making them unable to voice the same questions she would ask without hesitation.

Every bar, every pub, every cafe was full of backpackers and their singlets, shorts and thongs, their array of fading tattoos and face jewellery. We gave up after an hour and plumped ourselves into a furry hot-pink love seat in an air-conditioned bar where the small space was compressed by too much black carpet and chipped gold paint.

'We could be anywhere,' Josie shouted over the thump of 1980s retro pop.

'Okay,' I called back, my straining voice breaking mid-word like a pubescent boy's croak. 'Let's have this drink then go to the beach. Maybe the locals are skinny dipping.'

'Maybe they're swimming in their pantyhose.'

'What?'

'You can't swim with bare skin now. The water's full of stingers. You know, box jellyfish.'

'We can't swim? Crap, Josie. Why did you bring me here?' The love seat vibrated to the Eurythmics singing 'Sweet Dreams'. Every time I heard that song I'd think of my mum, stubby in one hand, spliff in the other, swaying on the grass on summer nights, slapping at mozzies and trying to make my little brother dance with her.

'I was lonely, Merry Merry. And this is my big trip. You have to do Cairns and Cape Trib on the big round-Australia trip.'

'Couldn't you have waited till you got somewhere with a proper beach?'

'No. Hey, listen to this.' She waved a brochure at me. *'If you happen to encounter a cassowary do not run from it. Face the bird and back away slowly until you can hide behind a tree or bush. Cassowaries live in rainforest remnants to the north of Cairns. The cassowary grows to two metres, as tall as a man. These giant blue and black flightless birds sport a large brown casque, or helmet, on their heads. Each muscular leg has three toes: the inside toe bears a long claw that resembles a dagger.*

While normally peaceful and shy, the birds will attack during mating season. The male cassowary is responsible for incubating the eggs and teaching the chicks how to forage.'

I nipped the brochure from her hand and opened it.

'It looks like the bird that time forgot. Let's go on a tour, Jose. Let's get on a cassowary bus with fifty other tourists and go discover ancient history.'

Josie said nothing. She'd been on the road for four months before she sent me the ticket. When I met her at the airport, I was shocked to see her lank hair and flat face. Her facial expressions were all wrong – it was as though her skin had thickened and couldn't fold and crease properly anymore. She'd eased up a bit now. She was laughing again. But she still wasn't the old Josie.

I finished my beer and set the sweating glass on the table. 'I'm going to do it, Josie. A touristy tour. You coming?'

'Nope.' She gestured to the waiter to bring another beer.

'What the fuck is going on with you?'

She fish-eyed me. The dead stare. 'I'm thirsty for beer,' she said.

'Shut up. Shut up with the bullshit and tell me what's going on.'

She closed her eyes. The thin skin of her eyelids was a dull mauve. I waited but she didn't open her eyes. Didn't speak. Her silence eddied around me. I felt the pull on my skin. I wanted to speak to fill the space of what she couldn't tell me. I wanted to ask about the boyfriend whose pictures had appeared then disappeared from Facebook. I wanted to say that her father called me every day for a month after she left and her mother had followed each call with a text of apology for bothering me.

'Fine,' I said. 'I'll do it on my own.'

Instead of taking a touristy tour, I asked at the hostel if anyone was going to the Cassowary Lodge, which is how I ended up the next day in a beige Camry Rent-a-Wreck with a Christian couple from Canada and a Taiwanese girl. They'd met at a postgraduate conference on world literature. This was their last day in Cairns. I was paying a quarter of the rental and petrol.

'So are you, like, a student?' The driver spoke without turning his head but I could hear him perfectly, his voice ringing through the car like the speech of a reverend or a salesman.

'No.' I didn't want to go on, but that would have been rude. 'I do contract work in the public service. The government.'

'Hey, that's great!' The girl twisted in her seat and pushed her left hand toward me as if we were about to do a high five. My hand was still sweaty, as was the rest of my body, moist and sticky from waiting in the heat to be picked up. I waved my hand vaguely in the direction of hers and mumbled, 'High five.'

'So, like, policy?'

'No, like, photocopying.' Those Canadians were prob-ably only two or three years younger than me, but they'd obviously never worked a day. Straight from school to university, conference trips across the globe, exciting adventures in cars with the locals who earned a living doing photocopying and filing. I turned to the Taiwanese girl in the seat beside me.

'What do you study?' I asked.

'I am professor,' she said, and turned to look out through the window.

I wished I'd taken the touristy tour.

Josie was lying on her bunk when I got back. I pulled off my clothes and lay down on the lower bunk in my underwear.

'We need better jobs,' I said to the slats and bulging mattress wads above me. 'And the cassowaries were in an enclosure and bored and they were as tall as men and looked angry. They're dinosaurs, living in the wrong time and the wrong place. We dinosaurs from the lost world all need better jobs.'

'Better jobs? I guess I got chosen by the wrong parents and went home to the wrong house. Then I went to the wrong school and I met you there and we both got the wrong jobs.'

'Wrong school all right. Wrong suburb, wrong country, wrong time. I never thought I'd say this, Jose, but I want to have a good job and a nice car and a house and … are we talking about the same thing?'

Above me Josie shifted position and the shape of the mattress through the slats rolled like the underside of a raft.

A hand reached over the edge of the bunk. I took the note-book and read.

J & M's Travel Diary, Day Three. I am having trouble telling Merryn that I found out I was adopted. And freaked. And left Melbourne. And everything is shit.

'Fuck,' I said. 'Fuck.'

So here we are, standing up to our hips in the dawn sea, dressed in bikinis and pantyhose. We're holding our arms high and she's gripping my right hand like she's the referee and I'm the winner of the bout. She's gripping my hand so hard it hurts, and I think of those years at school when all I wanted was to be her, the glorious, take-no-prisoners, bulletproof Josie. I can see the transparent blue of a box jellyfish drifting toward us on the lip of the swell, its tentacles performing a slow shimmy in the seawater. There are probably millions of broken-off tentacles here too, random strands riding the currents, wrapping themselves around the driftwood and the seaweed, the tiny silver fish and the human beings.

'I feel better now,' Josie says. 'The water is refreshing.'

My arms are getting tired. It's tempting to let them drop into the cool sea.

'Thanks for coming,' she says.

'Of course I came. I'd always come.'

Our raised arms start to tremble with the strain.

'I think I'll go back to shore now,' she says.

She lets go of my hand and leans over to kiss me on the cheek. The movement causes water to lap over the waistband of my pantyhose. I wait for the excruciating sting, but nothing happens. The jellyfish washes past me on the swell, its gelatinous body bumping harmlessly against my nylon-wrapped thigh.

'I'll stay in a minute longer.' I wrap my arms around my chest and stare out to the horizon, white-blue against the dark line of the sea.

Restraints

The labs should have been locked, but because of a massive power surge – followed by an outage – every room was gaping as if some angry foot had kicked open all the doors. Normally, the inside of the buildings was lit to banish any idea of a shadow. White walls and white linoleum. Windowless hallways and labs. Security points at every entry. Now the only light visible was the glowing green of the exit signs.

The other weekend skeleton staff were racing around the dark building like disturbed ants, panicking about damage to the instruments. I was hurrying too, not because anything urgent was going to happen in my lab, but it seemed wrong to stroll when everyone else was hysterical. At one point I turned a corner in the corridor, tripped and lurched several steps toward the bleeding green aura of an exit sign beyond the next bend, and had to press my hand against the wall for balance. When I tried to use my phone as a torch, the light was no brighter than the white of a playing card, so I put it back in my pocket.

My lab would be fine, but I was a little concerned about the test subjects in the animal house. Their restraints operated on an electric switch. If the restraints had failed and the monkeys pulled away from the caps now, the electrodes would be torn out of their brains and a full year of the team's work would be ruined. Still, I knew there were backup generators for the important machinery and electronics, and Jay was monitoring the animal house so he could lock the restraints manually if necessary.

Because of the lack of light, I overshot the door to my lab. The instant I stepped through the doorway I realised I was in the wrong room, but what I saw was so fascinating that I stepped further inside. This lab had light paths in the floor, like the lights that lead you out of an aeroplane in an emergency, and they gave off enough illumination for me to see more clearly. Unlike the lab where my work was taking place – a cross between an engineering workshop and an electronics factory, with half-finished parts lying around on benches and discarded finger prototypes cannibalised for the next version – this lab had a wall of full robot prototypes mounted on racks. While we worked on the single element of the hand grip, and the lab on the other side of us worked on limb mobility and the next lab calibrated vision, here you could see the progression of the full machine design. Usually we weren't allowed to see the assembled prototypes. Too much money was involved in this intellectual property. So we worked in our separate rooms, and the head engineers with full clearance put the robots together in the high-security lab. Our phones even had software that disabled the cameras when we walked through the security barriers.

The green light from above the door shone directly onto the prototype wall, giving the machines a golden-green glow like tarnished brass. The first version of the prototype was clumsy and large, essentially a rolling bot. Version two beside it was sleeker, leaner, multi-limbed. The next iteration began to look like some kind of creature rather than a simple robot. Four more versions along and you could start to see what this was becoming.

My head turned, almost involuntarily. It is movement that draws the eye first: something any prey knows. A cat knows, hunched and still under the azalea in the yard as the local terrier trots by. The deer frozen in the sights of the rifle knows. In the far corner of the spacious lab was a diamond wire cage the size of a squash court. Four machines were inside the cage. I thought I had glimpsed movement in the dimness, but now the machines were immobile, seemingly stuck to the wire in different positions. One hung from the ceiling.

I returned to examining the prototypes on the wall. The ones in the second row down had two legs shaped like chicken drumsticks with claws for feet, and a stumpy body covered in mesh. No head. Further along the rack the machines had gained another two legs. As I was examining them, my hand reached up to scratch my cheek and I caught again a flicker in my peripheral vision, as if my movement had somehow registered with the machines in the cage.

When I approached the cage, the robots did move, adjusting their positions. They were four-legged, with the same mesh-covered headless body as the prototypes, clinging to the wire with articulated metal feet, their grip possible because of the digits I had helped design. Inside the mesh of their torsos I could see glints of glass, perhaps eyes or cameras. Some kind of sensor. They were the size of large bulky cats. I had been designing robotic parts all my working life, but these machines were different, more like animals.

I stepped closer again, compelled to look. The machines travelled slowly around the cage. They each moved to a new position which would keep me in their view, like a team of hunting predators. I backed away, inadvertently knocking over a stool. At the clatter of the stool bouncing across the floor, the creatures – and I still think of them as creatures even though I know they were not alive, just robots – unclenched their feet from the wire and scuttled around the cage. The noise of them moving, the oily metallic clicking of their limbs and rippling of their mesh coat, the lack of voice or sound or smell other than metal and static, the swaying of the cyclone wire under their weight: all this was mesmerising. But it was my sensation of being stalked that let me know the monkeys in the animal house were still locked into their restraints, the electrodes were in place, and the brain–machine link was functioning. I could see the robots, and the monkeys could see me.

A moment later the lights came on. Once I had stopped shielding my eyes from the sudden glare, the eerie sensation was gone. I left the lab quickly, afraid someone would find me in there. I should have turned back to go to my lab, but I found myself walking to the animal house. The electronic pass at my waist beeped as I exited my building, and I crossed the white concrete path that led through the lawn to the house. I had never understood why we called it a house. From the outside it looked like a grey government building, squat and regular and unexceptional. Inside the foyer were, once again, white walls with white linoleum, but once you passed through the double set of doors, the colour of the corridor changed to the polished grey of steel, with basins and supply cupboards and doors with reinforced window glass along the walls.

As I reached the room where the test subjects resided, Jay pushed through the door, and it closed firmly behind him. I heard the automatic lock slide into place.

'Vin, mate, everything all right?' he asked. He was breathless.

'Yeah, yeah,' I said, aware of being out of place. 'You?'

'Bit busy. The blackout, you know. You're the fifth guy to come and check on the subjects. They're fine, except jumpy from sudden darkness and all the activity. Is that all?'

'I thought I'd drop in to see the setup again, you know? Nothing special.'

Jay sighed. 'I'd rather you didn't, Vin. It's all been a bit much. I'd like to let them settle.'

'I won't be long.'

I was insisting without knowing why. In the last year I'd only visited this room twice. Once, we had to ensure the electrodes were properly placed, so we brought down a prototype hand to test the stimulation-response while we observed. The second time was after staff drinks in the canteen, when the new assistant wanted to see the animals we were using. We shouldn't have come that time.

'Two minutes,' Jay said. 'And stay up this end of the observation window.'

The monkeys were in their specially designed chairs, heads clamped to keep them still, sensor caps replacing the detached brain pans. They looked well nourished. Their excrement was collected under the chairs and washed away by a steady stream of water, so the lab didn't smell as bad as you would expect. All this registered as I watched their hands clenching and releasing in a fashion that reminded me of my own aching hands flexing when I'd been locked in the lab, working at the computer too long.

'So the power failure didn't cause any disruption to the link?'

'No. Backup kicked in straight away.' Jay made a show of looking at his watch.

'And …' I said. 'Uh, I ah …'

I couldn't think of another question to ask. I moved a couple of steps down the room so I could see the monkeys' faces. They were stretching and squeezing their lips together, opening their jaws, squinting so their eyes were almost hidden. I moved a little further forward. I was almost in their sightline.

'Don't do that, mate, please,' Jay said. 'It's better if they get no stimulation here. You do enough stimulation from your end, okay? I'm just trying to keep the fucking things sane for another three months until you're done with them.'

My gut turned over, and for some reason I had a vision of my ex-wife with our Pomeranian in her lap. She liked to dress it up in dinky little coats with ribbons and bows. She would never clean up the dogshit in the yard because she said it was too disgusting. After she left I gave the Pomeranian to my mother, who said to me, *Don't bother giving me those stupid coats. Maybe it will remember it's a dog.*

I took one more step. The eyeballs of the monkeys rolled toward me, their heads constrained from movement. In the paper we had published about our research, we had named them Subjects A through D.

I wondered what the machines in the secure lab were doing at that moment.

A Short History of Peace

This house where we live was built for labourers four
centuries ago. The storey above us is empty already, the
tenants gone last week. The cramped rooms; the worn
stone where we step down into the kitchen; the bathroom
that juts out from the back wall of the original house where
once the workers sluiced water over their sweating scalps
from a hand pump in the yard; the patch of dark soil near
the back fence where the remains of old fires were tipped
by women when they rose at dawn – this house reminds us
of who came before.

Yesterday there was a knock on the front door. I told
him not to answer. He said there was no point. They would
come again.

My body too wears my history in its skin and its bones.
When I step down from the flagstone into the kitchen,
the past reverberates through my joints. I am corroded by
time and work and love, shaped into worn-down angles
and faint white scars that make me seem like a part of
the house, a stone woman who emerged from this wall

centuries ago. We are built of this country. The shape of our long narrow land repeats in our anatomy, split by the spine. The body has a left side and a right side but they are not in symmetry. They struggle for dominance. One generation we are left-handed, the next we are only adept with the right.

The human spine begins with the letter A, the atlas vertebra, which bears the weight of the head. The spine has twenty-six bones, some fused, some singular. In the bed where we lie together I trace his bony back, climbing the ladder in a two-fingered walk. Outside the room, delivery trucks for the factory down the road reverse with the insistent beeping that makes it seem as though they are travelling the length of the street backward. I wish I could hear that sound in my life, the alarm that says we are travelling backward. When travelling the spine of a country, or of a man, with one's eyes squeezed shut, it is difficult to know whether one is going up or down, forward or backward, into the past or into the future.

He stretches long like a cat on the white sheets and yawns with a faint yowl of tiredness. I can hear the click of tendons shifting into place over his bones. Two people walk past the front of the house, talking in bright loud musical notes. Their shadows traverse the blinds quickly, like hurrying ghosts.

It is dusk. The last of the sun is trying to slip into the house through the bands of the blinds. The air inside is heavy and still. We are too exhausted to talk anymore. All we can do is count the body. Listen to the body. Feel the slow measured wash of life through the circulatory system.

In the morning we sit at the table. The kitchen is in the dark part of the house, the north, with a window opening onto the side passage that traverses the west wall of the building and enters the small backyard beyond a rickety lattice gate. At different points along the route you can look inside and see what is happening to the residents.

If someone were to look in through the kitchen window this morning they would see him and me facing each other across the table with a pot of tea between us. There are books on the table, stacked at the end abutting the wall.

It is summer. We have an extra hour of daylight in the evening, and an extra hour of darkness in the morning. Right now the sun has risen and the heat is already radiating from the stone buildings. This is the fifth day of the heat wave. In a city accustomed to snow, we cannot cope. The tetchiness that started with our discomfort has escalated into panic and erratic behaviour.

The house has absorbed not only the heat but the smell of the heat. A whiff of rotting garbage and curdled milk, of the city unable to cleanse itself. The sour smell of overheated skin, of dried sweat, the dank water sitting in the bends of pipes. The deserted buildings, the drains, the abandoned dogs, the scorched leaves of trees, the nearly empty cafes on the boulevard serving jugs of iced water, the *thwomp thwomp* of distressed ceiling fans and the rumble of a few shop air-conditioning units straining and soughing and dripping their wastewater into grubby white buckets.

The morning light casts his skin in a papery hue. Almost transparent. Sometimes I feel as if I can see right into him, that his skin is tracing paper and all I have to do to examine his bones is press the skin up against them. Further inside are his organs, purple and maroon and crimson, shiny kidney bulbs and flaps of liver, the firm steady muscle of his heart. At night I hear his heart. The waves of blood beating through his body, the air whispering in and out of his lungs. He is still asleep when he rolls over and pulls me to him and his dry skin meets my damp hot body, weary from turning and tensing and fretting until even my cells are invaded with coiled strings of worry. He pulls me against his calm body and we enter the deep peaceful slumber that for a few years fell over our land.

Today he will go to the army. The same army that borrowed him for a year in his youth. They will ask him to remember the shape of a rifle in his hands. How to load the shells into a rocket launcher, how to focus his eye through the sights, how to brace his thin shoulder against the recoil of the machine. They are almost upon us, we are told. Knotted voices on the radio warn us to prepare. Our enemies want to destroy our short history of peace, split us apart again. Nothing will ever be the same.

I want to go instead of him. I want to pick up the rifle and press the stock against my cheek as I aim into the heart of my enemy. With my steady grip I would not miss, if only I could be sure who was my enemy and who my friend. I have examined the map of the human body, counted the fifty-four bones of the hands that hold a gun. In my surgery I have opened the mouths of other humans and peered inside, sewn their bleeding wounds into a purse of skin, pressed my fingers against their throats at exactly the point I would insert a knife to kill them. I do not know whether tomorrow those people will forget me, or provide sanctuary, or hunt me down.

He lifts the teapot and fills my cup. White cup, rosy black tea. Thick china. I hold the cup in both hands, my elbows en pointe on the tabletop like a ballet dancer's feet. The smell of the tea is bitter and even before I taste it I can feel the astringency on my tongue. We have no food here, no milk. The house is almost empty. We will abandon the last of the furniture and the books.

There is a knock at the door. His hand grasps mine across the table for a moment, our bones crushed together, then he rises. He shoulders his bag, his future and his past, the unasked-for weight of our nation's troubles. He is called by his people, I will seek refuge with mine. We will peel apart, the twin strands of DNA untwisting from the helix.

After the Goths

Before they were even in their bowling shoes, Cody started on the stories. He was talking about back when Dan was fifteen and he was fourteen, and his brother would swoop out of the house at night like a bat in his long black coat and smoky eyeliner. Around dawn, Cody would wake to Dan's footfalls along the hall and his bedroom door clicking shut, followed by the muffled thump of his clothes hitting the floor.

'Strike coming up!' Dan's girlfriend, Hannah, called out. She chose a pocked maroon bowling ball from the rack and balanced it on her upturned fingers. Standing with her toes on the line at the start of the lane, she swung her arm back and threw the ball. It bounced twice on the wooden floor before slumping into the gutter. Above their heads a cartoon figure popped up on the video screen and shouted, 'Bummer!'

Cody had a plastic bag with a change of clothes sitting beside the bench. His ticket and passport were in his pocket and his luggage was in Dan's car. In six hours he would be taking off to America.

'Did you ever wear the Man Skirt?' Cody asked Dan loudly. He turned to Hannah and his own date. 'I saw it in his room. *A symbol of our faith and our deviancy*, the label said. It had a "discreet zip fly" in the front,' he said, rolling his eyes and making exaggerated quote marks with his fingers.

Cody told the Goth stories more often than he should, but he knew they would always get a laugh. And those days were still so vivid to him, ten years later, that he could almost smell Dan's clove hair oil and the sweet scented wax of the candles burning in his room.

'It was a bit of fun. Not a big deal.' Dan spoke in a murmur directed at Cody.

Cody couldn't stop.

'What about the vibrating tongue ring? I always wondered which lucky girl you tried that on. Was it the fat one who used to recite death poetry in your room?'

Dan kept staring at the bowlers in the next lane as he sipped his beer.

Cody needed to say one more thing, and he needed to say it tonight, before he went away.

'She died the next year,' he told the girls. 'The fat one. She offed herself.'

'Oh my God,' Hannah whispered. 'How did she do it?'

'Whoa,' Cody's date said. She opened her mouth as if to go on, but closed it again. After a moment, she walked to the ball return rack and picked up bowling balls one after another, testing their weight, while the others kept talking.

'Wrists,' Dan said. 'Do we have to talk about this?'

'How old was she?' Hannah asked.

'I really would rather talk about something else,' Dan said.

'Okay, sorry.' Cody pulled his wallet from his back pocket and checked the notes. He asked if anyone else wanted hot chips, then went to the food counter and watched the girl shovel chips from the bain marie into a cardboard cup. She had black painted fingernails and a thin plastic serving glove on one hand. The nail of her index finger, filed to a sharp point, had pierced the end of the glove. It seemed like everything here was meant to remind him of Dan and the Goths.

The video screen was blaring out an old-fashioned marching tune when Cody got back to the lane.

'You should have seen Dan's fingernails,' Cody told the girls. 'There's a girl at the counter with nails like he used to have. His were much longer though. They were painted black but the polish would peel off like sunburn, and they clicked against each other when he tried to hold the cutlery. After a while he gave up. He picked up pieces of food in his claws and dropped them into his mouth like he was feeding a seal. My dad called him The Vampire.'

He kept going, describing Dan's friends, the hangers-on, who called him Daniel, but pronounced it Daarniel. They used to clank as they walked with their dull metal jewellery and buckles and ornamental zips weighing them down. In summer the black clothes must have been stifling, but they never wore another colour.

Often Dan wouldn't come home for meals at all, but when he did arrive he would sit opposite Cody at the dinner table, pale and hacking away at the cough he had acquired from smoking thin black cigarillos. Their father would ask Dan how school was going.

'Fine.'

'Still topping the maths? I don't know where you two boys got that gene from. Your mother and I can barely add one and one!'

'Back then,' Cody leaned over and said to Hannah while his date stared at the pins, preparing to bowl, 'Dan's hair was halfway down his back and he spent hours washing and conditioning it. I could never get into the bathroom. Even Mum complained. He had more make-up in the bathroom cupboard than she did.'

'Cody,' Dan said, 'that's enough, mate. It's your turn. Let's bowl, okay?'

Cody strolled down to the head of the lane and balanced the ball in both hands, mimicking the stance he'd seen people take on American TV shows. Then he backed up ten paces, swung the ball in an arc behind, and slid his feet down the runway to the lane, making sure that when he released the ball his left knee was bent low and his right foot pushed back and to the side for balance.

'Dude!' the video screen shouted, and a lairy tune burst from the speakers under the bench. 'Steeerike!'

'Hey, Dan,' Cody said when the commotion had died down, 'couldn't do that in a Man Skirt, eh?'

'What is it with you?' Dan's voice rose slightly. 'You can't let things go. You should try on a bit of make-up yourself, mate. Maybe you'd loosen up.'

In the next lane a girl bowled a strike and the winner's tune rang out again. Her friends screamed. The pack of girls milled around the lane, their glittery low-cut tops shimmering in the video light.

Cody had tried on Dan's make-up once. He caked on the white foundation and black eyeliner and watched himself from the corner of his eye in the mirror as he poked around Dan's room. He found condoms and crystals and small plastic packets with traces of white powder. Cocaine? But Cody was afraid to rub the powder against his gums like they did on television, in case it was something else, some Goth poison. He found black candles, a test tube with a crust of dried red liquid, bits of bone and fur and hair tucked into a jar.

Downstairs, later that evening, Cody told his mother that Dan was performing satanic rituals in his room. She tried to hug Cody and tousle his hair.

'Dan's going through a difficult time,' she said. 'And soon you'll be going through it too. Let him be, hmm?'

'I'll never do that dress-up stuff.'

'No, I guess you won't, sweetie,' she said. 'But there'll be something, you'll see.'

One of the things Cody found in Dan's room was a poem by the fat girl, written out in big loopy handwriting. He had heard her through the wall a few nights before, reading it aloud to Dan. After she finished the poem there was a long silence, when Cody wondered if they were kissing.

'Wow,' Dan had said finally. 'Heavy poem.'

Cody hid the poem and a few other things he had taken from Dan's room in a box at the back of his wardrobe.

Dan failed school that year. The week before classes started again, he threw out his make-up and his jewellery, sold the big coat to a kid down the road and cut off his hair.

Dan's repeating meant that he and Cody were in the same class. They sat at opposite ends of the classroom. For the first month of term, Dan's Goth friends floated past the classroom window staring in at him, trying to attract his attention without showing any of the life or enthusiasm that might ruin their image. The teacher made mock-tragic faces at the class and they giggled while Dan flushed pink. He never acknowledged his old friends in their black clothes and soon there were no more Goths in the school. His group, once they had shed their make-up and costumes, blended back so smoothly into the school population that the whole Goth thing might never have happened.

After Dan's friends took off the Goth clothes, the fat girl was the only one Cody kept thinking about. She was not hugely fat, only plump, with big thighs and breasts. She carried her fat in a defiant way. Her favourite clothes were tight short skirts and chunky shoes. When they passed in the corridor she stared at Cody, daring him to acknowledge her. So he did, even though he preferred to avoid Dan's friends. He gave her the slightest of nods. More an upward tilt of the head than a nod.

Another day she asked Cody if he knew what they were supposed to be doing for biology homework.

'Dunno.'

'My name's Jenny,' she said.

He gave her the head tilt and walked away. He knew her name.

She still came around to visit Dan for a while after the Goth time. Cody could hear them murmuring through the wall but they had music playing and he couldn't make out what they were saying. In the long silences when the murmuring stopped, Cody lay on his bed and imagined Dan putting his hand up the girl's short skirt and tugging down the white undies Cody had seen when she bent over at school. He could picture Dan's hands on the girl's breasts, her big round breasts, kneading them and pushing them, his tongue in her mouth.

Halfway through the year, Jenny stopped visiting Dan. But she'd still stare at Cody at school and he'd still give her the tilt, until one day they ended up sitting together at lunch and they swapped a mandarin and an apple.

'Hey, Cody, over here,' Hannah called from the back of the bowling lane. She pressed her finger on the electronic scoring screen.

'Look. The scores aren't right. Did, um, did your friend miss a turn?' She whispered in Cody's ear, 'I'm so sorry, I've forgotten her name. Say it next time you talk to her.'

Cody's friend was from his work. It was only when she arrived at the bowling alley that she realised it was a date.

'Where is everyone?' she'd asked as Dan and Hannah went off to hire shoes. When Cody told her she was the only one from work invited, she had sucked her lower lip for a moment, and said, 'But aren't you going away for a year?'

And now, when Cody turned to say her name, he was too late. She was already busy at the counter, changing into her outdoor shoes. She came back to pick up her handbag.

'Thanks for the game and everything, and good luck on your trip. I don't … I … Yeah, anyway, have fun.'

Aware that Dan was watching, Cody leaned down to kiss her goodbye, but she ducked and stepped off. Her dark hair swung like a metronome as she walked away. Her buttocks were two high sexy mounds pushing up and out in turn with each step. At the door she turned and waved once.

Cody stood watching the automatic door that had closed behind her. 'She reminds me of that girl from school we were talking about. Dan, doesn't she remind you of her?'

'Not the one who died? Was she your girlfriend?' Hannah touched Dan's arm.

'No, she was a friend. It was Cody who went out with her.'

'Not really,' Cody said quickly. 'We just did it a couple of times, you know, like you do in high school.' He kept staring at the door, wondering if he'd ever see his date again.

'What was that Goth girl's name again?' Dan said. His look at Cody went on and on like a mile-long freight train in the outback, loaded up with enough stuff for ten towns. Cody felt himself start to redden.

'Can't remember. Hey, Hannah, come on, it's your turn.'

When she was out of earshot, Dan turned to Cody. 'Yes, you can.'

Hannah bowled a strike. She screamed and ran halfway up the lane and back again and the attendant saw her and spoke over the PA: 'Please stay off the lanes. Off the lanes.'

Cody watched her run back to Dan, fling herself on the bench beside him and kiss him on the mouth.

When Dan had taken off his Goth costume, the hard, superior shell fell away from him. Their mother had said to Cody, 'See, I told you he'd get over this silly phase. I suppose it'll be your turn next.' But Cody never had a phase. He waited to feel something different in himself, but nothing seemed to change.

The next time Hannah went to get drinks, Dan said to Cody, 'Look, I think it's really good you're going on this trip. You can relax, have a laugh. That Goth stuff, mate, I'm so sick of hearing about it.'

'I did try on your make-up, you know.'

'Cody, are you listening at all? I don't care.'

'That girl told me she was going to kill herself. I'd fucked her twice and I told her to piss off. I didn't believe her.'

'Is that what this is about? She told us all a hundred times she was going to kill herself. None of us believed her.'

'I just do the Goth jokes to make people laugh. I'll stop, okay?'

'Cody, it was ten years ago. Let it go.'

'I have let it go,' Cody said, frowning.

'It wasn't your fault.'

'I know that.'

Hannah had brought back beers and she stood beside them, slopping dregs on her shoes.

'Anyway,' Dan said, 'no one could have stopped her.'

When they finished the round of bowling, Cody gathered his things. Hannah drove. They sat in silence as the car sped down the garishly lit freeway to the airport.

'It'll be brilliant, mate,' Dan said, slapping Cody on the back as he headed toward passport control. 'Take care. Don't do anything I wouldn't do.'

Cody remembered how his face had looked in Dan's make-up. He had seen his blackened eyes and white face in the mirror and hardly recognised himself. He'd imagined going out to a club and being someone else, just for one night, but the thought scared him and he had washed away the make-up so quickly that the soap got into his eyes and his mother asked if he'd been crying.

At last his plane was on the runway. It began to pick up speed. Cody felt his body being pressed gently into the back of the seat.

'Jenny,' he said.

The passenger in the next seat shifted to face away from him and leaned her head against the shuddering wall of the aeroplane.

Family Reunion

There was a party when I first came to this country. The table was heavy with plates of pizza and chicken balls and Turkish dips with sticks of celery that no one touched. Balloons clustered on the ceiling, trying to escape the heat of the room. A badly lit fire in the fireplace sent out curls of woody smoke, and a heater with two red coils sat burning in the opposite corner.

'This is my Filipino brother-in-law, Enrico,' Alan said each time he introduced me. At that point, the person I was meeting would clap my shoulder. 'Welcome to Australia!' As if they had all rehearsed this gesture in preparation for my arrival.

'I told everyone all about you,' my sister said the first night, before the party, before the bad feeling entered the house and hung around like the shrivelled party balloons that her husband keeps forgetting to take down. She said this in English, loudly, so that he would hear from the next room.

'I told them how you used to call me Bibby, and how sad you were when I had to go to another country

79

to find work. You cried on the phone and begged me, "Bibby, please come home." And I had to tell you to get off the phone and put Mama on the line, that Mr Kelly was paying for me to call from Hong Kong and he would be angry at a little boy in the Philippines wasting his money.'

My sister, grown old now, with creases between her breasts when she presses her hands together in the prayerful gesture of joy I remember so well, turned her head away from me and called out, 'That's what I told them, didn't I, Alan?'

He harrumphed like an old man then called back, 'That's what you said, darling.'

I may be Bibby's little brother, but I am now forty-six years old. I have been married and I have two boys, young men now, who live with their mother in the small town where she and I met and married and lived happily for the twelve years I worked in the mine. When the mine closed and I moved away, like the other men, to find work in Manila, my wife and I lost the closeness we had found through shared meals and worry for our children. I would go back to visit and find her distant. Polite, always. Kind. But distant. When I tried to be a husband to her she lay stiff and silent with her legs straight like a wooden doll in the bed. I am nothing more to her now than the provider of money. And that is all right. We lost too many years apart. How can I expect love from her when she doesn't even know how many teeth I have left in my mouth?

My sister, Estrella, told me to come to Australia because I can make a great deal of money.

'Alan makes sixty thousand a year and we get a car as well,' she told me. 'He has no trade, but he makes plenty of money with no trouble. It's a good life here.'

She sponsored me to come to live in Melbourne. Her husband signed an agreement promising the government he would support me if something happened and I could not work.

'Don't worry about that,' Estrella said. 'You'll find work straight away.'

How sure she has always been of everything. We believed whatever she told us when we were young. Even my mother obeyed Estrella. Estrella called from Hong Kong, where she cleaned floors and cared for her employer's huge empty apartment, and she told my mother to send all the money she had.

'I will make it double,' Estrella said. 'My boss is a stock-broker here in Hong Kong. He knows the Hang Seng. Send me everything.'

She made us some money. But at what cost? When Estrella was a young woman, before she left for Hong Kong to work as a maid, my mother would boast about how *pakipot* she was, always playing hard to get. She was a shy and modest Filipina. When she came back from Hong Kong the first time, she was no longer a virgin. She never said a word but we knew. She had to go back to Hong Kong because no one in our town would marry a girl who had been spoiled. For years she worked in Hong Kong as a maid until finally she met a tourist in a bar and they married. Mr and Mrs Alan Beasley.

I cannot say for certain what happened to Estrella in Hong Kong, but she changed. She learned the Chinese way of talking loudly and arguing. Now, she nags me, her brother only newly arrived here. She wants to know every detail of my day. I am a man, not a child! When she nags me like this I feel like I do not know her at all. She is no longer the loving sister I used to adore.

In Manila, I worked for a man who owned seventeen gambling parlours. My employment began at dusk when the stink of the streets grew stronger and men and women began to hurry home. Only the gamblers and the drinkers stayed out late in the parts of town where my employer's machines and tables could be found. I finished at dawn, usually exhausted, and I slept till late afternoon, when I would wash and iron my clothes, clean my apartment, maybe meet a friend for coffee before work. A simple, hard-working life.

I was not dissatisfied with my life in Manila, but I knew I could do better. And Estrella insisted that if Alan could make so much money, so could I. Then I arrived here and met the famous Alan. After our first meal together, Estrella sent us away from the kitchen. We settled side by side in front of the television, facing the screen, the bottles of beer in our hands growing warm and flat as we watched young men and women joke with each other and throw bags of cement about and pose and cavort in front of the cameras. We barely spoke. I was shy. Alan, I found out as we sat this way night after night, was being Alan.

Now, while Estrella is washing the dishes or tidying up after dinner and Alan and I are planted in front of another program on gardening or current affairs, we pretend to chat. I ask Alan a question, he answers to the television. He never looks me in the face. Estrella says it is the way of the Australian man. I think it is something else. It is only a month since I arrived and already my brother-in-law treats me like I am nothing. I wonder what Estrella has told him about me.

Alan works for the council. When I ask how his day has been he waves his hands in the air and complains about the people he supervises.

'I can't get them to do anything,' he says. 'They're lazy sods. Every report has mistakes. Half of them can't put a sentence together. They're always slipping out of the building for a fag and not coming back for twenty minutes.'

Alan is balding and has a small paunch that sags over the belt of his dark grey suit. As soon as he arrives home from work he hurries to the bedroom, then reappears in a pair of shorts and a T-shirt. Estrella brings beer to the back verandah, where we sit on green plastic chairs until dinner time, watching the magpies and blackbirds hopping around in the garden.

Three days ago, as we sat on the verandah in the chilly autumn air, Alan told Estrella that he would be getting a pay rise next month, an extra eight dollars in each week's pay packet.

'A promotion!' she cried. She jumped out of her plastic chair so quickly it tipped over and bounced along the verandah, and she rushed over and hugged Alan. He tilted his head back and she kissed him on the lips. To my horror, I thought I saw her tongue slip into his mouth. I turned my head away, feeling sick, imagining the mingling of their beery spit. I wondered, as I looked in the other direction at the next-door neighbour picking tomatoes from his garden, whether Alan was cupping her breast again, like he had done the other evening when she leaned over the table to pick up his dirty plate.

After what seemed like minutes they pulled apart. Alan patted Estrella's large bottom, bound in one of her colourful skirts, and she picked up her chair and sat down again.

'Sorry, mate,' Alan said to me. He rested his hand on Estrella's knee. 'We've got to respect your brother's feelings, sweetie. You know he doesn't like us having a cuddle in front of him.'

'*Sabali nga ili, sabali nga ugali,*' Estrella muttered to me before she lifted her glass of beer to her mouth.

Estrella always liked to spout proverbs at us when we were young. As the oldest child of a fatherless family she thought she had to educate us. Now I am a forty-six-year-old man and she is still trying to tell me what to do. She doesn't need to tell me that people of different countries have different customs. I know that perfectly well. But it does not mean we have to demean ourselves by behaving like them. Sexual relations between a man and his wife should be a private thing.

My mother told me many times when I was growing up that I must respect a woman's purity and innocence. She taught my sisters to be shy and modest. On the streets of Manila I knew plenty of women who thought modesty meant nothing. They made their money with their bodies. Now here was my oldest sister, flaunting herself like one of them.

Once Estrella had sat down, Alan gave her the bad news. 'Sorry to disappoint you, Stell, but it's not a promotion. It's just an indexed pay rise from the last negotiation.'

So this man, this weak man who watches his juniors wander away when they should be working, will get a pay rise. I saw this in Manila as well. Men earning more and more money in their jobs for no reason, drifting higher and higher like balloons.

Always I come back to the balloons. The balloons from my welcome party, still there in the lounge room, sticky with smoke from the fire made with green spring wood and floating on the bad breath of the three of us watching television night after night, are haunting me.

Every time I look up at their bald wrinkly heads stuck to the ceiling, I think of Alan. It is very difficult for me to believe he is only four years older than me. Like so many of the men I have met here, he is strangely soft. Not in his body, but in his manner. Always snuffling and coughing like an old man with catarrh. Always sitting.

Tonight we are not watching television together. I am here alone in the lounge room staring up at the multi-coloured balloon heads on the ceiling. Estrella and Alan have gone to the movies to see a romantic comedy like teenagers on a date. I think their problem is that they have no children. Estrella had almost given up on finding a husband before she met Alan in the bar in Hong Kong. She had written to me and my sisters that she would continue to work as a maid and send us money as long as her body held out, but that she was becoming older now. She said that the change had happened, which meant she could no longer have children.

I asked my other sisters what she meant and they told me that in our family the women's childbearing years end early. My sisters wept for Estrella that she would never feel the love for a baby of her own. I told them to stop their crying. Haven't we produced enough children for one family? I said to them. With eleven children between us, we should be happy that Estrella has only our children to spend her money on.

I have been working since the second week I arrived here at my sister's house. My first job was at a local bakery. I rose at two in the morning to bake the bread. I walked to work through dark streets where cats and dogs sniffed the damp grass and garbage trucks screeched and clanked along the kerb. The smell of the bread in the clean morning air was good. The pay was poor, though. I complained to Estrella because she had told me that her husband earned sixty thousand dollars per year and my salary was thirty-five thousand. She said I would have to wait a little while to earn more money.

I knew she was wrong. After a week at the bakery, I took the train to the centre of the city and I looked for the people I knew could use my skills. In Manila, I worked for a man who needed a helper with a level head. In Melbourne, such men were easy to find. Most businesses can use someone to explain to their clients why they must pay their bills. It is all a matter of attitude and I am composed and persuasive. If the clients do not understand my message, other people are sent who can persuade with more than words.

Estrella never asked why I stopped getting up at two in the morning. Two weeks later I handed her my board money and she looked at the notes in her hand.

'This is too much, Rico,' she said. 'We agreed one hundred dollars a week so you can save for your own house and bring your boys out here.'

'I am earning more than your husband now,' I told her. 'Keep the money.'

Estrella shook her head. 'You think this is a competition?' she asked. She rubbed her eyes with her fists and her mascara came off her lashes and lay in black sprinkles on her cheeks. 'So what are you doing that you can earn so much money so fast?'

'I looked up my old friend from Manila,' I told her, a little white lie but close to the truth. 'I am helping him with his business.'

'And his business is what?'

I was giving her the money, more than she had asked for. But was she grateful? No, not Estrella.

'His business is none of your business.'

'Of course it is my business. We are your visa sponsors!'

I refused to have that conversation. I knew Estrella was trying to make me feel guilty, to bring me back under her control, like when I was a boy and used to hang on to her dress so she couldn't get away from me. I shrugged and turned away.

'Don't ignore me!' she shouted.

Just like the old Estrella. I was sure that next she would start begging, like our mother used to do. First the shouting, then the begging. Hysterical female behaviour over nothing.

I was surprised when I felt her tap my shoulder.

'I thought you had changed,' she said to me, her voice back to normal.

'I know that you have,' I replied. It is not only Estrella. The way of being a woman has changed, I know that. Changed more than I can understand. And I know that I am supposed to change too, as a man. But why should I change? Why do things have to change and change?

'You must tell me where you are working, Enrico. It is for the government. We have to know.'

I started to walk away but she grabbed my shirtsleeve.

'Please, Rico. Tell me.'

I shook my arm but she was holding on too tightly. She began to cry and I told her to stop her stupid crying.

'I don't want you here,' she said. 'I don't want to be your older sister anymore. I am tired of this.'

I told her I would find a place of my own next week. I told her she was a stain on the family. First she brings me here, then she throws me out. What kind of sister would do such a thing?

She reached up and patted both my cheeks, as if I was a child. She patted them with more strength than I expected.

'Always, Rico, always everything was for you, the boy.' She patted me again, harder. My cheeks began to tingle. 'All the money I sent home from Hong Kong, all the toys and the food and the nice clothes. All for you. The special boy.' She was not patting now. Her slaps stung my cheeks. 'Your other sisters cleaning and sewing and working. All for you. And you do nothing except for yourself.'

'What do you mean? Didn't I go to work in the filthy Manila slums for my wife and children?'

She opened her mouth, then she closed it again without saying anything.

Now I sit here alone, looking at the withered Alan-head balloons on the ceiling, the sound of a laugh track coming from the television, and I wonder whether I should stay in this country or go home. I think of Estrella and Alan at the cinema, him pawing at her like she is a prostitute. I think of my wife, who asked me last year not to visit anymore, as if I am an annoying salesman rather than the father of her children. I think of that time long ago when Estrella was first in Hong Kong and I was allowed to talk to her on the telephone. I held the handset away from my ear, afraid that her voice would travel inside my head and get stuck there.

'Are you being a good little boy for Bibby?' she asked me, her voice all tinny and distant on the line.

Being good was simple then. I listened to my mother. I did my chores. I knew my place and what was expected of me.

So I told Estrella I was a good boy and she said that was all she wanted to hear.

The Word

A smelly old man in a greatcoat steers down the tram aisle toward Anna. She curls her fingers around her school uniform to edge the cloth closer and pull herself in tight, like an acorn with a hard shell. A tiny, unnoticed acorn next to the window. Something a smelly old man would pass by.

'Hey, sister,' he says in a thick voice.

She looks down. If she ignores him he might move on.

'I am the Lord Jesus Christ, come to bless you.'

The seats have plastic moulded rests but Jesus' bottom is bigger than his seat. When he thumps down he ends up jammed against her. He smells like urine and hamburger with fried onion. He has grey hair, greasy and long, and jagged nicotine-stained fingernails.

'Have you been saved?' he asks.

She keeps staring at her lap. Her heart pounds harder than usual.

The man's callused hand moves to her knee. She watches as if the knee belongs to someone else. Everything her mother has warned her about is stained on that big dirt-encrusted hand. She pictures it creeping up her leg. The other passengers turn away and concentrate on texting their friends and studying the newspaper. She half expects Jesus to grab her between her thighs, where Marco sticks his finger when they're at parties. Jesus won't put in one finger and moan like Marco does, his other hand busy in his own pants. Jesus will push his whole hand up her and she'll bleed and shriek and cry and no one will look at her because no one cares about anyone anymore, her mother says. The other passengers will pretend nothing is happening and hurry home to the television while Anna bleeds to death on the road.

But he doesn't squeeze her knee or knead it. He pats her kneecap, withdraws his hand and puts it back in the pocket of his greatcoat.

'Would you like to hear a story that happened to me?'

She shakes her head, meaning *no thank you* but unable to say it. 'Don't speak to them,' she imagines her mother saying. 'God, I should never have let you take the tram. I just wanted to save the environment.'

Jesus pulls both hands from his greatcoat and stands up. When the tram brakes he lurches forward, his arms flailing for something to hold on to. He staggers a few paces past Anna until the tram has stopped completely. If she squints at the window she can see in the reflection what Jesus is doing. She can't turn around and look in case he speaks to her again. He has caught hold of a strap with his left hand. His right hand is gesturing to the tram audience.

'I am the Lord Jesus Christ!' he roars.

Like everyone else she bows her head and pretends she hasn't heard. In school, the lesson about Jesus Christ was on a day when the teacher was in a stinking mood. Mrs Blacklock told the kids that Jesus was a good man who preached kindness. 'Do unto others as you want them to do to you,' she had said, or something like that. 'And read the Christianity chapter in your textbook by next week because you'll be tested on the Ten Commandments.'

Jesus lands beside her again. She's not afraid he will hurt her. She can see he's mad but he doesn't seem violent. He's just a mad smelly old man. 'Why didn't they leave them all locked up?' her father says whenever he sees a mad person out on the street. 'You call this social justice?'

Jesus starts up again as if he and Anna have never met.

'Girl, I am the Lord Jesus Christ. Have you been saved?'

This time she nods. It's another fifteen minutes to her stop. The stink is making her gag but the other passengers can't seem to smell him. She thinks longingly of the half-tab of E in her pocket. If she took it now, by the time she got home she'd be gone. Her mother would take one look at her eyes and start to cry. 'Good God, where did we go wrong? It's heroin, isn't it.' Whenever Anna comes home with cigarette smoke in her clothes her mother slumps on the couch and mutes the TV so she can moan louder. 'We've sheltered you too much, you know. We've overprotected you. You'll end up in the gutter—' 'Shut up, Mum,' Anna always says.

'When I went to the House of Prayer, they turned me away.' Jesus is so close to Anna she can feel his damp breath against her cheek. She's holding her own breath, trying not to take in the reek from his open mouth with its fleshy lips and stumps of blackened teeth.

'They turned away their saviour.'

Jesus rolls his eyes toward the roof of the tram.

'Cunts,' he says.

A shock jolts her. He said the word like it was any old word. Sometimes she whispers it to herself, in her bedroom. It's an incredible word for her. A word like a fist.

Once her father said it in front of her mother.

'Don't you ever say that word in the presence of our daughter,' she hissed, and spit flew out of her mouth. Anna ran upstairs and shut her bedroom door and muttered it all night.

'Cunt cunt cunt cunt cunt cunt.' She put her hands between her legs and said it under the bedclothes. 'Marco loves my cunt.'

The tram's now so crowded that there's nowhere to go. She'd rather walk than sit next to stinky Jesus. She lifts herself half off the seat to pull the cord but Jesus takes hold of her other arm and pulls her back down.

'Are you getting off?'

She nods. She doesn't feel afraid but she still can't speak. She doesn't have any words for this situation. She doesn't even know what to think.

'Will you take me with you?'

She shakes her head. The lady opposite has music buds in her ears and is gazing at an advertisement for holidays on pink and orange tropical islands. Anna reaches down for her schoolbag tucked between her feet. She edges past Jesus and threads her way through the crowd to the door, where she stands so close that her breath makes rapid patterns on the glass. Her house is still a long way away so she'll walk a stop or two and get on the next tram. A tram without a stinking Jesus.

It's only when she's crossed from the median strip to the footpath that she realises Jesus has followed her off the tram. Cars honk as he stumbles across the road against the red light.

'Hey, sister,' he calls. He moves fast for a man with flapping shoes. It's five o'clock, dusk, cold. The lights are glowing in the strange bright way they do at twilight. Soon her mobile will ring and her mother will whine at her. 'Why aren't you home? Are you out with that boy?'

'Sister!'

'I'm going home now,' she shouts back at him. 'My parents are waiting for me,'

'I was walking to the mount,' Jesus calls. His voice is burred with phlegm. 'A crowd gathered to hear me speak. Are you listening to me, girl?' He coughs then shouts again. 'I have things to teach you!'

Another tram sways past, glowing with light. Anna breaks into a trot. Behind her she can hear Jesus' laboured breathing and the *slap slap* of his broken shoe hitting the footpath. The cars on the road brake at the intersection up ahead and their red tail-lights are like alarm signals. His stink has got into her nostrils – she can smell it with each in-breath.

She could try to get into one of the cars, but there might be a murderer or a rapist inside. Her mother imagines Anna's brutal murder on a daily basis. She talks about all the ways Anna could be lured away by a stranger and killed as if all those TV shows she watches with murders and rapes and twisted plots are real.

Jesus is grunting with the effort of keeping up. He calls in a breathy voice, 'Sister, can you give me a dollar?'

'Yes, yes.' Of course, he wants money. Jesus catches up with her and waits as she drops her heavy schoolbag onto the ground and bends to search for her purse inside.

'You are the Samaritan,' he says. He touches her head with his hand and she wants to shake it off but she keeps on rummaging through the schoolbag. The smell of bruised banana drifts up from the open bag. Her books are lying on the footpath. Jesus leans close to her. What she at first thinks is a drop of rain drips onto her cheek, then she realises it is dribble from Jesus' mouth. Tears sting her eyes.

'Sorry, sister, sorry.' The hard skin of his hand scrapes once across her cheek, trying to brush away his spit.

A car pulls up beside them. A woman gets out of the passenger side. She leans back in and kisses the driver on the cheek, locks the door button and slams the door. As the car drives away she waves and adjusts her handbag on her shoulder. When she turns around Anna calls to her.

'Excuse me, I ...'

The woman stares. Anna looks across at Jesus standing on the other side of her schoolbag and thinks of children at assembly.

'Are you okay?' the woman says.

'Yes, but …'

'I am the Lord Jesus Christ,' Jesus roars.

'Yeah, sure you are, mate,' the woman says. She is older than Anna first thought. 'Come and walk with me, love.' She stretches out her hand.

Anna stands there with Jesus making soft grunting sounds beside her and her books scattered on the footpath and all she can hear banging on in her head is her mother's voice. 'It's not that I think people who call you "love" are common, like *my* mother used to say.' And her father commenting from the lounge room chair as usual. 'That's your mother, the champagne socialist. As long as they're not in her backyard.'

She rubs her face with both hands trying to wipe the images of home from her mind. As if he has been waiting for her eyes to be covered, Jesus clamps his hand around her arm, crushing her school blazer with whatever he has on his filthy hands.

'Begone, Satan!' he shouts at the woman and breaks into a coughing fit. His hand stays welded to Anna's arm. His whole body shakes from the coughing and Anna begins to shake too.

'Oh shit,' the woman says. Cars stop and start in a jerky stream behind her as the intersection lights change.

'I was going to give him a dollar,' Anna whispers, even though Jesus can hear everything.

The woman nods. 'Listen,' she says in a gentle voice to Jesus. 'I've got ten dollars.'

'Thy money perish with thee!' Jesus thunders, his other hand grasping the air as if he's trying to pull down the sky. 'The gift of God cannot be purchased with money.'

Anna's notebook has blown open and Jesus' foot is grinding into the page where she's written her night's homework. She needs to go to the toilet. It's dark and the three of them stand in a pool of yellow light from the streetlight above. Spit glistens on Jesus' lips.

In the distance the windows of another tram appear like a magic lantern. Jesus bends down and pulls the chemistry textbook from her bag. He brandishes the fat book at the woman before he lets go of Anna's arm and throws back his head.

'Father, why have you forsaken me?' he wails to the sky.

He draws back his arm and hurls the book into the traffic. It slams onto the road in front of a taxi, which brakes and skids. The car behind honks long and loud until both accelerate away, the one behind still honking and the sound receding like a siren. Jesus begins to mutter what sound like verses from the Bible.

She remembers the E in her blazer pocket and wishes she'd taken it before. It would be kicking in now. She'd be feeling warmer, and her teeth would be starting to clench with that delicious sensation of tightness. The gold of the lights would be more golden. A wash of happiness would spread through her body. If the E had already warmed her body, she would reach over and take Jesus' hand and say, 'It's all right, Jesus. We care about you.' She would love this woman who's stopped to help her, and she would love Jesus, even though he stinks. She would twirl around on the black footpath and sniff a great breath of the sour night air like it was scented with summer jasmine.

'Come on,' the woman says.

Anna bends down to push her books back into her schoolbag. On the roadway the chemistry textbook has been torn apart under car wheels. A few pages of formulae drift along the footpath in the wake of passing cars.

'Leave the books,' the woman says.

But she can't. 'Do you have any idea how much it costs to pay for your schooling and the uniform and the books?' her mother says whenever she complains about school. 'Just thank your lucky stars we didn't send you to the local high school.'

She scoops the books into the bag. Tucked inside is her Hello Kitty purse. Before she lifts the bag, she empties the coins from the purse and holds them out to Jesus on the flat of her palm.

'Suffer the little children to come unto me,' he calls, his arms wide, waiting to embrace her.

'I'm sorry,' she says. She slips the coins into his pocket, then steps back and heaves the schoolbag to her shoulder.

The tram rocks toward them with its familiar whine.

'Go! Catch this one,' the woman says. She gives a push and Anna takes off at a run, pounding along the footpath, her bag banging against her back. She makes the next stop just in time to swing up on the tram and looks back to see the woman walking quickly away. The Lord Jesus Christ stands alone, arms at his sides, hair hanging over his face, greatcoat trailing on the ground. He lifts his hand to her one last time and she presses her palm against the glass in reply.

When she gets home her mother follows her up the stairs, demanding to know why she's late. Anna slams the bedroom door behind her and hides the E for tomorrow night. Marco's sent her a text but she doesn't want to read it yet. She plugs her music player into the speakers with the volume as loud as it can go, and she lies flat on her back on the bed, still in her school uniform. Her breathing is shallow and her heart skips fast, then slow, then fast. Music roars around her like a hurricane. There might be some sounds outside her door, a mother shouting or a phone ringing, but that doesn't matter.

'Cunt cunt cunt cunt cunt,' she shouts, flying with the music. 'Cunt cunt cunt cunt cunt.'

One Good Thing

'If you were my sister,' I asked Klara Fuchs, 'do you think we'd still be best friends?'

'Oh, Natalie, of course we would,' she said, and I believed her.

We were in love, the way that primary-school girls fall in love with each other. When I look back now I realise that Klara was thin and brittle like a bunch of sticks held together with cloth. But at the time I thought she was perfect. She wore bright striped dresses that her mother had made, and matching single-colour cardigans. She wore long white socks every day. She smelled different from everyone else, tart and spicy like an exotic fruit. The first night I stayed for tea at her house and they served me sauerkraut I recognised the smell. Sometimes, in school, we held hands under the desk. I remember the sensation of her hot sticky fingers entwined in mine.

I was an only child. Klara had a sister and a brother. Her sister was nine years older than us, almost an adult. She only ever spoke to us to point out how annoying we were. Klara's brother, Dieter, was thirteen. As much as I wished Klara was my sister and could live with me at my house, I wished Dieter was not her brother and that I had never met him.

If Dieter found a drawing we had done, he ripped up the paper. If he caught us playing in the mud, he smeared the mud over our faces. If he caught us at the swimming pool, he tried to hold us under. He might always be around a corner, so we had to speak softly. He might find the spell we had written to ward him off, so we ate the paper.

When I sat opposite him at the dinner table, smiling politely as I tried to chew my serve of sour cabbage and meaty sausage, Dieter watched me. He stared until my throat tightened and I couldn't swallow. He seemed to hate me for no other reason than sitting opposite him at the dining table and catching his eye. Klara sat next to me at the table, hardly letting anything pass her lips, as if Dieter was controlling her food intake. She carried herself in a hunch, and she shivered easily. The temperature only had to be slightly cool and Klara would start shivering. Or if her brother was nearby. Then she shivered too.

The times Dieter was around were the only times I wondered if I could keep on being Klara's best friend.

One Sunday Klara's mother and father took us on a trip to the Caribbean Gardens in a suburb a long drive away. Klara, me, Dieter and his friend from school. Fibreglass statues of animals rose out of dry garden beds like we were in a museum, and the sun beat down over acres of brown dirt and colourless rides and stalls selling hot jam doughnuts and sausages in batter. The parents set up at a picnic table with a tablecloth. They brought baskets out of the car boot filled with bottles of beer for them and cordial for us, stuffed cabbage rolls and thick, heavy cake smelling of honey. At the table Klara's father shook out a newspaper and held it in front of his face. Her mother stripped down to a pair of bathers, lay her towel on the dirt and settled down with a book and a sunhat.

'Why don't you go for a swim,' she said to us, nodding in the direction of the muddy lake a few hundred yards away. A paddle steamer ploughed through the water on the far side. Klara and I wandered around the statues of elephants and giraffes and crocodiles. Further along the shore a replica submarine rose out of the dust like a grey dinosaur. Dieter was on the deck, trying to climb the periscope. Klara saw what I was looking at and she tugged me in the opposite direction.

'Let's play over there,' she said, pointing at a bare patch of earth further along the shore. I followed her and she picked up a big stick and started sketching something out on the ground.

'What are we playing?' I said.

Klara looked over my shoulder and whispered, 'Nothing.' She dropped the stick. She whispered again, 'Let's go and play over there,' and she pointed even further away, out into the field where even her parents couldn't see us.

'Are we allowed?' I asked. My parents would never let me wander that far. I glanced behind and saw Dieter coming toward us with his friend, red-faced and crying, staggering behind him.

'Okay,' I said to Klara and we started to walk quickly away.

'Hey,' Dieter shouted.

We bolted like startled deer, running till our breath was ragged and our chests sore. We ran past cages of monkeys and stands of poplar trees and enclosures of emus in the sun until finally Dieter gave up following us and we found ourselves in a small copse of eucalypts somewhere in the back of the Caribbean Gardens. We sat on the ground, cool earth covered in a dry carpet of leaves. I felt as if I had travelled through some barrier to reach a place in another time or another dimension. The trees had seemed small in the distance but now they were huge above us. I lay back on the fragrant leaves and looked up through the branches at the distant pale sky.

'Have we lost him?' Klara gasped, almost sobbing trying to get oxygen into her skinny body. 'Is he behind us?'

I sat up. She was still doubled over, still sucking in air.

'I can't see him,' I said. But that didn't mean he wasn't there.

He was there one day at their house when I rounded the corner, looking for Klara. He and another friend of his. His friends were always small boys, while he was big, solid, fleshy. His small friend was holding a dartboard and Dieter had a dart in his hand aimed at the dartboard covering the friend's stomach. They were in shorts, both of them, bare-chested. I wore a pink spotted dress and my best sandals because Klara and I were going to practise walking with books on our heads.

I never saw the dart leave Dieter's hand, never saw it fly through the air. I was watching the board to see where the dart would land before I made a break for it and ran across their line of vision on my way to the back door. When the tip of the dart flew straight into the boy's chest, above the right nipple, and hung there, I was as silent and astonished as both of them. We all watched the dart standing straight out from the boy's chest as if it had hit a tree trunk or a pole. Four feathers, vanes quivering. A brass collar holding the dart tip to the shaft.

A trickle of blood emerged from where the tip had penetrated the boy's chest, and dribbled down toward the dartboard he was still holding against his belly. All of us silent, waiting for the dart to fall out. Dieter let out a sharp bark, a laugh of sorts, and his friend's eyes widened as though he had only just realised that this dart was embedded in his own chest. The boy shrieked. Long and high like a rabbit.

Dieter won't like that, I thought, my stomach starting to spin. The shriek went on and on. Dieter's mother came pelting out of the house. Klara's narrow, frightened face appeared at her bedroom window.

'He moved,' Dieter called to his mother as she flew past. 'He shouldn't have moved.'

When she reached the boy, Dieter's mother took hold of the dartboard he was still pressing against himself like a target and flung it to the ground. The boy kept staring at the missile standing out from his breastbone. He pushed Klara's mother away when she reached for the dart. His mouth was wide open but no more sound came out. She stepped forward, grasped the dart, pulled, then covered the place it had come from with her hand.

A few weeks later I came to Klara's house and the boy was there with Dieter again. They were tying red crackers together and lighting the fuse before they threw the bundle into an empty oil drum in the vacant lot beside the house. The crackers hammered around the drum like a machine gun. Dieter laughed and laughed, and the boy with a hole in his breastbone stood behind him and giggled and glanced around nervously, as though the danger might come from somewhere else, not right in front of him.

'Go and get the Catherine wheels,' Dieter said.

'Okay,' the boy answered breathlessly, and as he raced past me to the house I wondered how Dieter could keep these people coming back.

When Klara and I were eleven, her family moved to a small farm in the country. The next summer holiday, I went to spend a week at their new place. They lived in a fibro house, and the property ended on the boundary of a flat scrubby national park. In the heat of the day Klara and I walked together through the straggly bush and sat with our legs dangling in the creek. Or we lounged on her bed in her bedroom, batting away mosquitoes in the dense air and slurping fast-melting blocks of flavoured ice.

Klara sat with her arms wrapped around her legs, her chin resting on her knees. Sometimes she held her pillow like a shield, pulled tight against her shins. She was so thin and could make herself so small that the pillow almost hid her from my view when I lay on the other end of the bed. When she was hidden away like that, she told me some of the dark thoughts that occupied her mind.

'I picture myself dead. Like I'm dreaming, it's so clear. My body lying bleeding on the floor, my head smashed in. My stomach split open like a supermarket bag. Do you ever have those dreams?'

'No,' I said.

'Dieter will kill me one day. I know it.'

She turned the jam biscuit she had been holding for fifteen minutes around and around in the palm of her hand and finally nibbled the jam that had oozed out the side of the biscuit. A red spot stuck to the corner of her mouth.

'I think he's insane,' she said.

Since she'd moved away Klara had sent me notes and cards. We'd talked on the phone but she had never mentioned Dieter.

'I haven't thought about him all year,' I replied. 'Where is he?'

'He's been staying at a friend's place. He's back tonight. I don't want to see him. I don't want him to live here,' she whispered.

'Neither would I,' I said.

We were silent for a moment. I picked at a mosquito bite on my shin and from the crater a drop of blood welled up. I blotted it with my hanky.

That night Dieter arrived. The car dropping him off pulled up so fast at the front of the house that pebbles from the driveway flew up and pinged against the lounge room window. The car door slammed and the car backed away, tyres spinning and crunching on the gravel.

'Let's go to my room,' Klara said hurriedly. She took my hand and pulled me out of the lounge room and along the hall to her room. Behind us, the front door opened and a gust of wind burned along the hallway.

On my last day at their house I woke late. I was sleeping on a mattress on the floor of Klara's room. The night before, we had set the alarm to twelve for a secret midnight feast of chips and chocolate we'd been hoarding all week. Everything tasted extra salty and extra sweet by torchlight. We stifled our laughter by stuffing the sheets against our mouths and fell asleep again at two.

'I think she's in the shed, darling,' her mother said when I came into the kitchen after my shower, so I skipped to the shed and pushed open the big door. Dieter and Klara were both inside in the gloom.

'Hi,' I said, unable to see them properly, 'what's happening?'

Dieter giggled his squeaky unnatural giggle. My stomach leaped inside my ribcage and my skin prickled. As my eyes became accustomed to the dim light, I saw Klara standing against the wall, her arms held out horizontally, her face turned away from Dieter, who was standing a few metres back from the wall. Below her hemline Klara's legs were glistening, and there was a puddle in the dust at her feet.

'Ready?' Dieter cried, and he giggled again.

Klara pressed her face back further against the wall as Dieter drew back his arm and flung a knife in her direction. The knife thudded into the wall above her left arm before clattering to the floor. Another was embedded in the wall near her face.

I tried to scream but no sound came out. Dieter was staring at me and giggling with such hysteria that he sounded like a neighing horse. I ran toward him and shoved as hard as I could, and he lurched back, dropping his handful of mismatched kitchen knives on the dirt floor. His laughter stopped. Instead, I could hear the furious rasping of his breath. He grabbed my arms and forced me backward until I slammed into the shed door and it swung shut. The only light came in through the green translucent sheeting on the roof. Dieter's face above mine shone green like his eyes. Even his teeth, bared in a crazy grin, looked pale green. He forced me to the floor and started to pull at my jeans.

'Klara.' My voice came out like a long, high sigh.

Dieter pressed his forearm on my throat and leaned down hard while he wrestled with my jeans with his other hand. I was choking. I punched him with my fists until he slapped my face so hard I thought my head would fly off my body. As I lay stunned with my head in the dirt, he rocked back onto his heels. He took hold of my jeans and wrenched them off, dragging my sandals along with them. Then he pulled open his own jeans. Now I screamed. His hand came down so fast to cover my mouth that only a peep escaped.

He was too strong for me. I tried to throw myself to the side, but with one hand still over my mouth he caught my wrists and pinned them to the ground above my head. He used his knees to prise apart my thighs and he pushed and pushed and pushed until something broke and he was inside me. The pain split me in two. His green face was inches away from mine, sweaty and grimacing. His teeth, still bared, were tipped with foamy saliva like a dog's fangs.

As everything slowed down in my mind I rolled my eyes from side to side, trying to escape the face leering above me. When my eyes reached their lowest point of vision I saw Klara's corduroy sneakers. I looked up. She stood, with her arms hanging at her side, watching. She was watching me, my face, and she stared and stared and I stared back, our eyes locked, expressionless, as Dieter pounded into me, grunting and panting. Finally he shrieked and let go of my mouth and my hands. He pushed himself off me, stood up and walked out of the shed, doing up his jeans. The shed door stayed open a crack and suddenly nothing was green anymore, just dull grey, back to dull grey.

Klara stood above me and held out her hand to help me up, but I turned my face away from her.

'Go away,' I whispered, the tears starting. Pain in my face, my throat, between my legs, my wrists. Moisture dribbling from inside me onto the dirt floor. I felt the cold on my bare thighs, the goosebumps rising, the hairs standing on end.

Klara moved slowly to the door of the shed. She hesitated there, her hand curled around the edge of the door.

'Get out,' I whispered. My throat seemed to have closed. Words could barely escape.

She waited a few seconds more. Then she pulled open the shed door and the light savaged my naked skin.

'If you tell,' Klara said in a scratchy voice like an old vinyl record, 'he'll kill me. You know he will.' She pulled the door shut behind her.

Twenty years later, that scratchy voice spoke behind me.

'There are seats here.'

A slim hand beside me pointed to a bench at my table, which was littered with chip packets and a dozen glasses – half empty, ringed with dried foam, lipsticked and smeared with oily fingerprints – from the crowd that had headed out to the beer garden. The funeral was over. Everyone had moved on to the informal wake at the pub and the drinking and shouting was getting harder and louder.

'Natalie?' the voice said into my ear. Her fingers touched my wrist, light as fairy dust, and twenty years vanished. I was flung back to the days of Klara, the hot sunshine and tickly grass, our special jokes and the purse full of lucky white stones we collected from each corner of the playground, chanting as we went.

When I turned I half expected to see the old Klara, her earnest eyes gazing into mine, reedy brown hair wound into the tight plaits that boys at school felt compelled to twitch and pull at every opportunity. Instead, there stood a woman with a blonde bob and smooth made-up skin. She shook her head and the hair followed in a perfect feathery swing.

'What are you doing here?' I said.

My chair rocked on its wobbly legs. Klara gave me some answer about a connection to my cousin's funeral as I tried to steady myself with my feet but found them jarring against the stubby carpet. A waiter came to collect the glasses and litter from the table. Once he had left, glasses in a ladder up his arm, the surface was still tacky with spilled beer and wine so that the underside of my arm peeled away from the table's veneer like a strip of contact.

'Natalie and I were at primary school together,' Klara explained to her husband. 'But my family moved to the country and we lost touch.'

I stared at her.

'We used to be best friends,' Klara said.

'I came to visit you after you moved.' I had to raise my voice against the clamour of the mourners. My glass was empty. Acid biting into my gut.

'Did you? I'd forgotten,' she said, tilting her head, still alert and birdy. She leaned sideways so that her shoulder rested against her husband's chest. 'Natalie was one of the smart ones at school. She's probably a doctor now, or a lawyer or something.'

'I stayed at your house for a week.'

She shook her head as if this was unbelievable to her. 'I've got a terrible memory,' she said. 'Haven't I, darling?'

'You always remember where the credit card lives,' her husband answered.

'That's because you let it live in my purse,' she replied smartly and laughed.

Of course she couldn't be like the old Klara. The discord was a kind of relief. This was not Klara. This person wouldn't know the answer to the elephant riddle that used to make us laugh until we got a stitch. She wouldn't know anything about us, or what happened.

On my last day at Klara's house when we were twelve I eventually made my way back to the house. As I stumbled through the hot dry kitchen Klara's mother asked me what had happened. 'I fell over,' I told her, and she asked if I was hurt and I said no, just a bruise. 'Are you sure, sweetheart?' she asked me. I said yes I was sure. She told me I should change my clothes and have another shower because I had dirt all down my back and in my hair and she didn't want my mother thinking they hadn't taken care of me. The hot water of the shower hurt me in every place. Afterwards I sat on the bed in Klara's bedroom, wet hair dripping onto the eiderdown, waiting for my mother to arrive and take me home. Klara came and sat beside me. I was too exhausted to push her away. Klara's mother put her head around the doorway and saw us sitting there side by side.

'Oh, you darling girls are like a pair of beautiful dolls,' she exclaimed.

Until that day I'd thought Klara was like a doll made of porcelain, that she was the one who would be easily broken.

'I'm going to get another drink,' I said to Klara and her husband.

I wouldn't come back to the table. I would pretend to fall into conversation with someone on the way to the bar, then slip away home to try to gather everything close again.

'I'll have a G and T. Give Natalie some money, darling.'

'No!' I said too loudly. I pushed myself out of my seat and rushed into the crowd of people roaring and jostling elbows around the serving counter. Once I was surrounded by other people, I began to feel better. At the bar I ordered a shot of whisky and downed it on the spot. Above me, the racks of glasses jittered in time with the jukebox bass. I ordered another whisky and moved further along the bar, out of Klara's line of vision, holding on to the counter with my fingers resting on its damp sticky towel because my legs were still shaking.

'Natalie!' A man in a grey suit with his tie loosened and his sleeves pushed up emerged from the crowd. He leaned across the bar and ordered himself a beer and me another whisky. He looked me up and down as if he was appraising my value, as if I was a piece of real estate.

'You're looking good,' he said. He rigged his sleeves higher up his arms. Rolled his neck before he picked up his beer and drained the glass. He knew I was a likely chance.

Klara and her husband were waiting at the other end of the room for me to reappear with a gin and tonic and amnesia. My cousin was burning to ash and bone in the crematorium. As the noise around me pulsed in shouts and raucous laughter I sucked in fast desperate breaths, giddy with the unreality of it all. The only reality was Klara, sitting at a table in that room. Klara wearing peach silk. Klara all grown up. I didn't want her to be Klara, but she was.

On my way back from the bar with a gin and tonic and another whisky, the muscles in my neck tingled and released. The third shot was fanning through my bloodstream.

'We thought you'd run off,' Klara said, glancing at her husband.

I raised my fourth shot to my lips and swallowed. 'Not this time. How is everyone, anyway?' My voice rode the hubbub, a punchy voice filled with green light and dust.

'We've left Rhiannon with a babysitter. We hate parents who take their children to every inappropriate event, don't we, Squidge?'

Squidge, as she obviously called the husband she had introduced as Lawrence, nodded. He was nursing the same glass of wine he had first brought to the table. Klara nestled up to him again. He smiled as she turned back to me and lifted her glass. The straw bobbed up and down in the fizzy tonic and she followed it with her pursed lips like a baby seeking a nipple. At last she caught the straw between her lips and I saw the old Klara for a moment, focused

115

intently on her drink, frowning. I would have recognised her anywhere, but I was surprised she had recognised me – it was as if she'd left little Klara behind on that dusty property.

'I meant the people I knew. Your family.'

Her face rippled, almost imperceptibly. It was the second sign of the Klara who had been my best friend so many years ago. I used to see that deep quiver when Dieter walked by, or when we heard his voice from another room.

'Oh, Mum and Dad have moved to Queensland. Dieter's married. Has his own salon now. Helen's still teaching.' Her eyes blinked, empty, while her hand travelled around her husband's lap like an animal searching for somewhere to hide. 'What about your family? I can't remember – did you have any brothers or sisters?'

'Salon?' I said. Did Klara remember our pretend salon? I would lie on the bed while she smeared my face with yoghurt and stained my lips purple with the juice of a cherry.

'He's a barber. He likes to call his shop a "salon".'

A laugh hacked out of my chest. 'They let him near people with a razor? Does he still throw knives? I hope he got better at it if he does.'

Klara and Squidge stared at me. Then Klara dropped her gaze. She picked up her purse and began sorting through its contents.

'Sorry?' Squidge said, speaking directly to me for the first time.

'Dieter loved to throw things at people. Sharp things. Didn't he, Klara?'

She pressed her lips together and shook her head slowly, looking down at the table. Her blonde hair flared in the light. Both her hands had delved inside her purse now.

'Did he? He was a terrible teenager, I suppose. I told you I had a shocking memory.' She looked up at Squidge. 'Didn't I?'

'Dreadful,' he answered. 'Completely vague.'

I had to close my eyes because I couldn't stop staring at Klara's features, trying to find the girl I had loved so deeply. We used to lie beside each other on the spongy surface of the playground and count each other's freckles. I would watch as Klara's bottom lip pressed briefly under her top teeth before she spoke. I thought it made her look like a mouse, a sweet, hesitant mouse. Sometimes I stood in front of the mirror trying it myself, but it never worked for me. I looked like a dumb rabbit. It was the shape of Klara's face and her mouth that had made her so loveable and vulnerable.

I rubbed my eyes till they stung, trying to superimpose one Klara on the other.

'I should get you home,' Squidge said to Klara.

'Yes,' she said. 'Yes, please.'

When I opened my left eye she was looking back at me. The blue of her eyes was like the sky shuddering behind a copse of wind-torn trees.

When I opened my right eye she was looking back at her lap.

I touched her arm. Her thin white arm.

'Klara,' I said. I didn't know what else needed to be said anymore. I tried our old call sign, one of the secret codes we used together. 'Time flies like an arrow.'

'Very nice to see you, Natalie,' she replied. She was supposed to say, *Fruit flies like a banana*.

Squidge stood and stretched, the bones in his back cracking.

I took Klara's hand in mine. I wanted to have the sensation of our damp childish hands clasped together under the desk one more time. But her hand was dry. Under the skin I could feel the tremor of her bones and muscles, a tremor that probably never left her.

'I'm glad you made it,' I told her softly, so her husband didn't hear, so there was one good thing left between us.

She stood. Her husband held out his hand to help her and she took her hand from mine and gave it to him like a princess taking the hand of the groom from the carriage step.

'Bye,' I said.

'Bye,' she answered.

Once, we were like sisters. But we were not sisters. She has a real sister and a brother and they are her family. And she owes me nothing.

Deja Vu

One wall of the room with the sulphur spa was glass, and Anthony arrived early each morning so that he could slip into the warm water right next to the window wall and look out, down the hill, at the view of the small French village of Llo and its surrounding mountains. If he came late there would already be a cluster of crepe-paper old men in the bath, snorting and complaining and arguing as if they were drinking Pernod around a table in a cafe, not undergoing a cure at a medicinal hot spring. At the height of their gesticulations, the old men's hand slaps landed *crack* on the water, creating little tidal waves that lapped over the rim of the pool and spread across the red tiled floor. But if Anthony arrived early enough, only he and another man, a quiet old man, used the pool. They sat and watched the mist rise off the silver fields on the mountains opposite, and the people hurrying to work in the village below, and they kept the silence.

For three days in a row Anthony had shared the bath with the old man and watched him leave when his wife came to get him. She arrived each morning at eight fifty-five, according to the misty clock on the wall. She always walked straight up and tried to peer through the one-way glass into the baths, cupping her hands around her face and looming up in front of the two of them like a seal nosing against the glass of an aquarium. The old man would wave back at her, pull himself out of the bath and pad off past the ornamental palm to the men's changing room.

On the fourth day Anthony slept in. At lunchtime he was sitting in a nearby cafe when the bather's wife stepped in through the entrance. She made an exclamation that sounded like a squawk as she surveyed the tables. She's like an old chook, Anthony thought, but he kept watching her anyway, oddly fascinated. The woman was wearing a large floppy hat of aqua terry towelling that completely covered her hair and partly obscured her face. Her upper torso was quite slim and she swivelled like an office chair on her heavy hips as she looked around until she had found a table to her liking. Then she pointed to the one she had chosen and, still pointing as though her levelled finger would keep the seats in existence until she arrived, pushed her way through and sat down. She had already examined the menu by the time her husband reached his chair.

'You'll have *café au lait*?' she said.

'No, I think I'll have a beer,' he answered. He reached over and took the menu from her.

Anthony, watching surreptitiously, noticed the old man's hand quiver as he held the cardboard menu. Despite his casual air, the man was quite frail.

'*Un café au lait et une bière Kronenbourg, s'il vous plaît,*' the woman said to the waiter. '*Une bière,*' she repeated after the waiter had walked back to the bar. '*Une bière, une bière.* I'll never get that "r" sound. *Une bière.*'

'He understood. I don't see a problem,' her husband remarked. He kept perusing the short menu.

The first time he saw them, Anthony had guessed they were English. It was the man's long face, and the woman's hat, and her expression: discomfort or anxiety, the look of a displaced person. He wondered if English people had always looked this way or if it was something that happened when the empire crumbled. From the corner of his eye, he saw that the woman was making her way to his table, carefully arranging the four chairs in her path to form a corridor as wide as her hips. He slid the postcard he had been writing under his book.

'Do you mind?' she asked as she sat down next to Anthony. 'I saw the book and I thought, well, he's either English or speaks English, so we really should introduce ourselves. I'm Alice. That's my husband, George.' She beckoned to George, who got up and walked languidly, like a movie star, through the chair corridor toward them.

'We were dying to speak to someone in English,' Alice said. As she looked around and saw the waiter standing at the table she and George had left, she made the odd, squawking sound again before calling him over, '*Ici, ici!*'

'Anthony.' Although he wished the couple would leave him alone to his book and his silence, he had never been able to speak rudely to anyone. 'I've seen you over there, looking at that building. And of course,' he nodded at George, 'in the bath.'

'Our son designed that building, Anthony. Martin's an architect. He's designed buildings all over Europe, hasn't he, George.'

George nodded, and shaded his eyes to look across at the building.

'He always makes the doors too narrow, though,' she went on. 'You couldn't fit a pixie through some of Martin's doors. In his house, it's a lovely house but— Oh, there's Madame Larouche.'

Madame Larouche was a small figure under a white parasol, climbing the steps of the complex across the road.

'She's French, staying at our hotel, taking the cure. She's taken a real fancy to me, I can't say why,' Alice said.

George turned his head to gaze at Madame Larouche.

'She's very kind, does absolutely everything for us. And she lives in Paris. Paris! Yoo-hoo, madame!' Alice stood up and waved at Madame Larouche, who eventually saw her, waved back, and kept walking.

'Well, what do you think of that! Now she's ignoring us. She's on the hot-spring cure for her arthritis. Of course, you're too young to be on the cure,' she said, looking directly at Anthony for the first time. Alice's oversized glasses emphasised the smallness of her features, each delicately in place like petits fours on a plate. Her mouth held the shape of a drawstring purse.

'No. I'm here on the cure, too.' Anthony shifted in his seat.

'Arthritis? A strong, young man like you? Why, you can't be over thirty.' Alice's eyes scanned what was immediately visible of Anthony's body, the tanned arms and prominent collarbone.

'Actually, insomnia,' he answered abruptly, trying to head off more questions.

The conversation halted. Anthony lifted his empty coffee cup and pretended to drink.

'Your son's not with you?' he asked Alice after a few moments.

'Oh no. As if Martin would come anywhere with me. No, we came to see the building and George thought he'd enjoy the baths. We knew he'd have doors like that again, though. His signature doors, they say, don't they, George. I think it's because his wife's so tiny. Even in their magnificent house they only left the external doorways the original size. They built a granny flat for us on the side. Completely separate of course. A young couple need their peace.' Alice's lips grew tighter, as if someone had pulled the drawstring.

'Yes, it's a good house and a lovely flat,' George said. He smiled at Anthony, but Anthony couldn't read anything into the smile.

'Should you be drinking coffee if you're an insomniac?' Alice said. She reached over and placed her warm hand on Anthony's knee. 'Let us buy you a cup of tea.' She swivelled and called the waiter. 'Monsieur! Monsieur!'

'No, thank you, really,' Anthony said. 'I must—'

'Do you walk, Anthony? George walks. He's an amateur geologist.'

'Is that right?' he asked George, then looked behind Alice to where the terrace cafe ended and the mountainside seemed to grow up out of the floor. The tiles of the cafe floor matched the basalt colour of the rocky mountainside, but there was no mistaking where one ended and the other began: up from perfectly even square tiles reared the jagged blocks of stone that characterised the whole mountain range. Every morning an attendant would be out here first thing, sweeping away the soil and rock and leaf matter that had drifted down the night before.

'Yes. Where you find these natural springs in the mountains, you'll also find some fairly interesting volcanic formations,' George began. 'It's really quite astonishing how you can look at the surface of a piece of land and work out what's happening underneath. Why, I—'

'George, we'd better let young Anthony get on with his book. You know how bored people get with your rock talk,' Alice broke in. She had already taken money from her purse. 'Do let us pay for your coffee, Anthony. It's been such a pleasure to meet you.'

Anthony watched her trudge away to negotiate with the waiter, who seemed to be pretending not to understand Alice's French. After she had paid and started walking with George down the road to the village, Anthony's shoulders dropped. He slipped the postcard out from under the book and picked up his pen. So far, he had written the date. He scribbled, *Dear Mum, today I met someone you might like*, then decided to order more coffee.

The next morning Anthony was stretching out in the warm bath and watching the hairs on his legs drift like seaweed under the water when George slid in beside him.

'Morning, Anthony.'

'George.'

George rolled his head back against the lip of the bath and sighed.

From the other rooms of the complex, Anthony heard coughs and wheezes, the thwack of oiled hands against skin in the massage room, a couple of women talking about the hotel where they were staying. The soft splashing of water and the hum of people's voices carried through every room. Anthony lay with his eyes closed, listening to the surface murmur, and the rumble of the pump machines under the complex. Even when he felt the water curl around his body because George had stood up, he kept his eyes closed. Alice would be outside the window now, trying to peer in. Or she would be clomping up to the front door of the building to wait. She would always be there, Anthony thought. Like that rumbling sound of the pumps under the floor, you would always know she was there.

The following day Anthony sat hidden in the shade of a cafe awning, watching the passers-by, many of whom had become familiar in this small town of people taking the cure, walking the mountain paths, eating at the same restaurants and hotels. George sauntered past on his own and turned off at a sign that pointed to a hiking track. Half an hour later, Anthony was startled by Alice's voice.

'George is out on a walk. I can't make it up those hills with my hips. Rheumatism, you know. How are you feeling, Anthony?'

'Fine, thank you.' He flipped over the postcard his pen had been poised above, the same postcard he had been trying to write for days. The picture showed a deep chasm that ran the length of the mountain range. Anthony had taken a bus tour along a road that wound along the top of the mountains, directly above the chasm. At a photo stop, while the other tourists lined up for pictures and broke out crackers and fruit from their travel bags, he had stood at the far barrier of the carpark and stared down at the fast-flowing river that churned and eddied at the bottom of the chasm. He had imagined himself in the water, being thrown about, dashed against rocks, tossed up and sucked down again like a leaf. He had felt the same sensation people feel at the edge of a sheer cliff – that momentary desire to let go and fall away.

'I must admit my hips are aching right now. It's the damp,' Alice said.

Anthony closed his book as Alice sat down. He slipped in the postcard to mark the page.

'Reading again, Anthony? I don't like Agatha Christie but it's all they've got in English at the hotel. My son reads a lot. He and George often talk about books. Of course,

Martin never mentions what he's reading to his mother.' She picked up the menu, glanced at it, then put it down. 'Still, he's a grown man.'

Alice's sly complaints made him want to shout, to start up from his chair and stand over her, to smack her, all things he would never do. She made his head ache as though all the words he wanted to shout were dammed up in there. He thought of her husband, the silent partner. Did George have the same feeling when Alice prattled on like this?

'It's your first time here, Anthony?'

'Yes.'

'Ours too, but I don't think we'll be coming back. It's quite a tiny town. If you're not taking the cure there isn't much to do, is there? George has worn his own personal path over the hills. I'd like to go with him if it wasn't for my hips.'

'Perhaps you should take the cure,' Anthony said. Not that it was working for him. As if a warm bath could cure anything. As if travel could take you away from the persistence of memory.

'Oh no, not me. No, absolutely not me. Madame Larouche from our hotel is taking it. A lovely woman. Quite taken with me, I can't imagine why. Now, I wonder if George is back at the hotel yet. He might be waiting for me. Yes. I'd better go. Anyway, Anthony, you must have dinner with us tomorrow night. We've found an excellent restaurant and we'll be leaving the next day. It's the Le Clos. We can meet you there at eight.'

Anthony declined. Alice insisted. When he finally accepted, she laughed with delight and told him how pleased George would be to have a proper, manly conversation.

'We've had Madame Larouche and a Spanish woman following us around everywhere, but George is tired of them. He needs a man to talk to. And I can see you're lonely.'

After another restless night and a day spent avoiding the places where he thought he might run into the couple, Anthony arrived at the restaurant to find them already seated.

'My hair,' Alice moaned, fingering the drab frizz that had previously been neat, artificial curls. 'It's the humidity. I was almost too embarrassed to come out and see you tonight, Anthony, but we were so looking forward to it.'

'I won't take a photo then,' Anthony said. He feigned a gesture of putting away a camera, and in the pocket his fingers brushed the dog-eared corners of the postcard he had been trying to write to his mother.

George began to smile at the camera joke, then slowly leaned way back in his chair and performed a long, almost soundless, wide-mouthed laugh.

'We'll have some wine,' Alice went on. 'That'll help you sleep, Anthony. It's shocking a young man like you having trouble sleeping. I've been worrying about you. Oh, here's the madame who owns the restaurant. We met her last week. She loves the English.'

Anthony's teeth were clenched. When he tried to smile a greeting at the owner of the restaurant, his face grimaced. He was longing for the food to arrive so that his mouth could open and busy itself with chewing, then this night would be over, and these people would be gone. George sat in the chair across from him, admiring a photograph in an ornate gold frame on the wall behind Anthony, although his eyes kept straying to Anthony's face. Anthony was beginning to despise the way George stayed mute under the incessant, appalling chatter of his wife.

'Seen any interesting rock formations?' he asked George while Alice ordered the *prix fixe* menu for the three of them.

'Actually, I was walking along the peak, where the path to the cemetery goes, and I spotted an outcrop that looked rather interesting a short way down the south side of the hill. You'll never guess what I found.'

Anthony nodded to encourage him. Alice had finished ordering and was listening.

'Coming out of the rocks, up there where no one goes, was a natural hot spring. Of course, this is a volcanic area, quite volatile under the surface, so these things are common, but I couldn't believe it hadn't been tapped, not in a tourist area like this. There it was, trickling from a cleft in the rock, still warm.'

'He was so excited about it when he came back to the hotel. I'd been waiting for hours and I hadn't eaten since breakfast …'

'I didn't say I'd be back early,' George said quickly.

'Yes, but you didn't say you'd be late either. I thought you might come back for lunch so I—'

'I did not say I would be back for lunch.'

Alice tossed her head, then smiled at Anthony.

'I'm so hungry,' she said. She patted her hair again and tried to plump some curl back into it. 'Do your parents live in Australia, Anthony? Are they well?'

The waiter arrived with their bowls of soup and a plate of bread.

'Did you drink the water, George?' Anthony said, after a mouthful of the potato soup. He sometimes wondered if the cafes in Llo kept aside their blandest dishes to serve up to the English.

'It had a strong taste, earthy, plenty of minerals. Not hot, but warm. I wanted to put some in a container and bring it back for Alice to taste. Unfortunately I had nothing suitable with me.'

'I couldn't have drunk it,' Alice said. She slid her spoon into her soup plate and pushed both away from her. 'Something warm that bubbles up out of the ground? No, I couldn't drink it.'

'Why not?' Anthony asked, genuinely curious.

Alice pushed her plate further into the middle of the table, plumped her hair, shook some pepper into the discarded soup, then into George's soup, which he was still eating.

'It terrifies me to think that hot liquid is seething and bubbling right under our feet,' she said in a quavering voice. 'That the ground under us is just a thin crust. Those terrible

130

earthquakes where people fall into great cracks that have opened up in the earth! I can't understand why George is interested in those things.'

'It's my hobby,' George said, and he stretched back in his chair for another eerie, silent laugh.

'I'm glad there's no mirror here. I'd hate to see my hair.' This time Alice plunged her hands into her ragged hair and dragged them through, pulling out strands caught between her fingers. She stared down at the hairs tangled around her fingers, then looked up and around the room.

'What a lovely dress the madame has. So French. So …'

Alice gazed down at the table again, at her hands and the hairs twined loosely around them.

'The main course is taking so long, and George is tired from his walk. Of course, there isn't really much else to do here.'

Her eyes had widened behind her big glasses, and now she glanced at George. He reached over and patted her hand, and when he pulled his hand back to lift his spoon, a single grey hair lingered on. Once more he looked up, past Anthony, at the aerial photograph of the mountains around Llo that showed clearly where once, long ago, the crust of the earth had torn open and spewed molten lava across the plains.

'Alice has trouble sleeping too,' he said. 'And Martin, our son. He can't sleep either.'

Anthony lifted a mouthful of the floury soup to his lips. The warm metal of the spoon clicked against his teeth and he shuddered. Was it the taste of the soup, he wondered, or the click of metal against his teeth that had given him deja vu? He knew Alice was about to speak. He almost knew what she would say. Or perhaps he didn't. The feeling was gone before he could test the truth of it. Even while he was thinking about the deja vu, it had fallen away. Always, that sensation. The falling away. The possibility of falling away.

Breaking Up

Two days after the windows imploded, the first cracks appeared in the walls. We had taped up the glassless windows with gaffer and cardboard and at night the wind moaned as it nudged the torn edges of cardboard, trying to get in. The sky was a murky grey but electricity still coursed through the powerlines. I peeked out the front door. All the houses in the street were lit up like casinos. A neighbour I'd abused for letting his dog shit on our lawn crouched on his roof hammering something down. He saw me looking at him and he waved but I stepped back inside and closed the door. This was no time for socialising. My husband, Mattie, lay on the couch, exhausted from gathering shards of glass and heaping them into empty suitcases.

'Why?' I said.

'Just trying to keep things together,' he muttered before he nodded off.

We collected all our foodstuffs and laid them out on the benchtop in the kitchen.

'Why did you buy so many tins of tomatoes?' Mattie asked as he stacked the tins in a small mountain to the left of the coconut milk and the baby corn. 'And how many smoked mussels did you think we could eat?'

The next day rats and cockroaches and ants and spiders fled the house. They gathered in a lumpy carpet on the roadway and started moving toward the sea. Cockroaches rode the humped backs of rats while spiders climbed over each other in their hurry to escape. Our dog roamed the neighbourhood, baying and howling. He raided the neighbour's rubbish bins and brought back their tax returns.

'I hate knowing this much about them,' I said to Mattie.

'Too much. We know too much about each other,' he replied.

Before long the cornices tumbled from the walls and the doors refused to shut. Amazingly, power still travelled through the wires and we watched movies to try to bring back the good old days. Mattie chose *The Towering Inferno* and I thought he was joking but we sat through the whole thing laughing because it was so bad. Then I picked *The Poseidon Adventure* but we didn't laugh anymore and I knew I'd gone too far.

'You always go too far,' Mattie said, knocking back another glass of the Grange we'd hoarded for fourteen years. He fell asleep, drunk, and I made a fruit cake.

'We should call people,' I said, so we called everyone we knew. Every day. We tried to think of new conversations to keep them liking us. Maybe we tried too hard. Maybe we smelled desperate. They stopped answering our calls, so we stopped answering theirs. We picked up the phone to shout into it. 'Breaking up. Can't hear you. Breaking up.' I added a few crackling noises.

I tried looking on the internet for recipes with tinned tomatoes. The page stalled when I got to casseroles. A message told me the server had crashed under an unusually high load. Then one of the walls groaned and the bookcase fell on the computer so it didn't matter anyway.

When a brown goo began to seep through the floorboards it stuck to our shoes like tar and walking became difficult. I tried scraping it up to fill the cracks in the plaster. It worked for a while, then the goo dried and crusted over and fell off like scabs.

We were playing our favourite old music now. I danced to 'If You Could Read My Mind' and I shimmied up and down the stairs until the banister came away in my hand and I toppled onto the couch beneath the staircase.

'Soft landing – it's your lucky day,' Mattie shouted. 'Maybe we do have a chance! Let's open a bottle of champagne.'

I was tired of shifting furniture to cover the holes that had appeared in the walls, and the roof had fallen into the bedroom, so I lay under the kitchen table for a nap. The brown goo tar was comfortingly warm. Mattie passed me down a plate of crackers and the last of the smoked mussels and a glass of Dom.

'To us!' we toasted as the light fittings shattered and the fridge powered down. We couldn't light the candles because we'd given up cigarettes years ago. The evening wind carried a giddy sweet-smelling gas and soon afterward the distant wailing of sirens ceased and there was no more sound except the hiss and rend of our marital home folding inward.

Recreation

So the text message came at lunchtime and I went to the hole in the wall and got out cash. You don't know it's happening until the day. A text message arrives on your phone, giving you the location and the hour. They don't take credit cards yet but they're so organised I wouldn't be surprised to see one of them whip out a machine sometime soon. Thirty bucks to get in, minimum bet is twenty. There are blokes who lose a thousand a night. I take along a hundred bucks or so. I win, I lose, it's no big deal.

At eight thirty I headed off in the good car, the 1970 Torana I restored myself. Born the same year as me but in much better shape. One day I'm going to compete the hill climbs in that baby.

I told the wife I was going to the pub. She's called me on the mobile a couple of times during a fight and asked what the shouting's about. Drawing the meat-tray raffle, I tell her. She can't hear the animals in the ring because they're too busy surviving to make noise.

First time I went I was nervous. I thought the place would be full of thugs with knuckledusters in their pockets. Once I got inside I felt better. The blokes might have knuckledusters in their pockets but most of them looking after the gig are kind of weedy and smaller than me, so I reckon I could take on one or two if anything started. Not that I'm any great shakes as a fighter, but I learned basic street fighting with the Broadie Boys when I was a kid, and I'm pretty sure it would come back to me. We had some real bust-ups back then. Makes my teeth ache to think about them. I can't remember much except running down the street with blood pouring out of my mouth or my forehead while the hard kids stayed behind to finish it.

I never see those guys anymore. A couple of them are inside. The smart ones like Matt are in real estate. We see him drive through my estate in his Mercedes coupe and my wife asks me where I went wrong. She's only kidding. Me and my good mates ended up in trades and physical work. I could have been a plumber, but I got one sniff of the dunny pipes and gave up.

Funny – what I'm doing now probably stinks just as bad but it only earns a quarter of what a plumber gets. Still, it's the kind of job that doesn't stretch the mind. It pays the bills, and I don't spend nights worrying about work or doing the books. The money appears in my account every fortnight, and nights and weekends are for me and the family. I've got a wife, two girls and a dog of my own. He's a nice dog, a heeler. The big thing in his life is a walk in the park, rounding up his dinner and then a lie-down on the couch.

Those animals in the ring, they're something else. They're not like any dog I've ever known. It's obvious they don't think about about chasing a ball or begging for food. They'd take out your throat before they'd beg. That's one of the things I admire about them. They're all pride and power. The way they surge into the ring, eyeball the opponent while the handlers are doing their best to hold them back. There's a bloke at my work in the factory-cleaning business, Vic, he reminds me of those dogs. Vic looks at you as if you're some kind of inferior being. He takes no shit at all from the boss who's this puny kid, the son of the owner, university degree in management. University degree in poncing about, Vic calls it.

Last week we're scrubbing ceilings caked with three years of gunk, the shit raining down on us, and ponce boy calls out, 'Don't forget the vents, guys!' I ignore him the way I usually do, but not Vic. Vic puts down his long-handled scrubber real slow, then he goes down the ladder off the scaffold and he turns around, smooth and tense, a hunter stalking his prey. Ponce boy's shitting himself. Even from up on the scaffolding you can see his Adam's apple charging up and down his throat. He starts to edge backward but the wall's in the way and he puts his hands up to say stop. He makes me think of a guy in a movie facing a gun. The only gun here is Vic. He's a loaded gun, and we're all waiting for him to go off.

As he gets within a few feet of ponce boy, Vic does a strange kind of a skip. If you were standing in front of him, you might have thought when he flexed his legs that he was going to spring on you. Ponce boy does this weird whistle from his throat as he opens his mouth as if he's going to say something, then Vic laughs and swings around and climbs straight back up the scaffolding. We're all staring at him. 'Don't forget the vents, guys,' he calls out to us in a high-pitched whiny voice and we all crack up. Haven't laughed that much in years. Ponce boy disappeared for an hour or two. Probably went home to change his trousers. The other blokes laughed as hard as me. They're good blokes, most of them, except a couple I wouldn't want to see too much outside of work. You can tell those two would be nasty drunks.

Vic's the hardest man I know. He doesn't get excited. He'd have no interest in the dog fights, where we're crammed together in a pack and the minute we see the blood a howl goes up, while the dogs, those incredible machines, are grunting and maybe growling a little, but pretty much they're silent. One rips a piece of flesh off the other, you can see the raw wound, the blood welling up like an oil strike, and the dog doesn't make a sound but half the men around the ring are crazy screaming soldiers.

Last night the location was outdoors, miles away from anywhere in an industrial estate, stacked containers looming over us, a few empty sheds, huge pieces of machinery parked along the roadside. It's always way out – Dandenong or Laverton or some new suburb I've never heard of.

The first fight was over in minutes and one of the dogs retreated with a torn-up leg. The next two came out. When they exploded out of their harnesses you could see this was a fight of champions. The man next to me threw back his head and made a gurgling, crying noise. He sounded as if his throat had been cut. I had to look sideways and check he was all right. Then the yelling started up and everyone was shouting and screaming and the dogs took it to the end. They don't always let them do that.

It was a clear night. The moon looked like someone had been at it with a pick and shovel. I stared at the moon and for a minute I wondered what I was doing there. I'm not a screamer. I don't usually bet a lot of money. But it's the feeling. That's what I realised. When the dogs are at it I'm so keyed up I can feel every muscle in my body pumped and ready for action. My whole body is one great big throbbing cock.

After the fight finished, the screaming tailed off and blokes swore and punched each other in the arms and shoulders as if they'd won the match themselves. As the trainer of the winning dog raised his arm in a victory salute, the other one walked out of the ring carrying his dead dog in his arms. I felt bad seeing the man with his dead dog, until he reached the cages where the dogs were waiting, leaned over and spat, and tossed the carcass aside like a side of beef. It sent the same thrill through me as when I'm watching a porno and the action gets a bit rough.

The third fight was different. We were drunk on the smell of blood. I couldn't stand still. No one could. My legs were twitchy and hard and I kept needing to shift from one leg to the other, do a quick jog on the spot. I'd lost fifty on the last fight but I thought just this once I'd go over my limit, put two hundred on the next one. Holiday pay was coming up in a fortnight. And the dog I was backing was superb. It waited beside its owner outside the ring, brindle, mad-eyed, foaming at the mouth. Probably drugged, but I'd heard most of them were. I ran to the bookie and threw my cash at him. Shitty odds – by that stage I didn't care.

The caller shouted to release the dogs and the crowd pressed into the ring. We were breathing hard and elbowing each other to try to get closer. The brindle stalked on stiff legs toward the other dog, a sorry-looking mutt with pink half-healed scars along its flank. It was taking too long. They should have charged at each other but as the brindle inched forward, the mutt began to back away. Its owner stepped in, picked it up and threw it toward the brindle. When it landed on four paws, nose to nose with the brindle, it lowered its bullish head, looked away, licked its chops. Cowered. Backed off again, belly to the ground. Useless.

'Stupid fucking mongrel,' the owner shouted, his voice barely rising above the noise of the men in the crowd, who were urging the animal on or booing or cursing at no one in particular. The owner grasped the dog under its armpits and dragged it forward until it was only a head away from the brindle. 'Fight, you cunt!'

I shouldered my way to the front of the crowd, the blokes around me swearing and telling me to fuck off as I pushed past. By the time I got to the rope, the champion dog had the other down. The one underneath was bleeding from a gash on its head and the champion was braced on those stiff legs, fangs bared, daring it to get up. It wasn't getting up. Its owner waited till the champion had been pulled off, then grabbed the dog by its hind legs and dragged it out of the ring. 'He can still breed from it,' a bloke next to me said to his mate. 'No he can't,' the other said. 'You don't breed from losers.'

I could never tell the wife about what I do on these nights. She's an animal lover. Gives money to the animal protection society. On the way home last night I stopped the car near the lake on our estate. I got out, drank a couple of beers and smoked a couple of cigarettes and stared at the water until my heart slowed down. I saw a dog loping past, some suburban mutt on a night prowl looking for cats or possums. It would never catch anything. My heeler's the same. Maybe he's descended from wolves but now all he's good for is lying around and eating tinned muck.

As I was starting up the engine to go home, a passing car gave a blast of the horn. I stuck my hand out the window with a thumbs up. Blokes around here love my car. Vic offered to buy it from me. As if I'd sell. Only other car guys understand. When I curl my fingers around the original leather steering wheel I bought at a swap meet last year and I rev the engine and worry about an oil leak I noticed on the cracked cement of the garage, it's like the car is alive and I'm looking out for it like a man should with his mates.

You've got to look out for your mates, I know that. But some of those guys at work, they get a few drinks in them, I wouldn't feel a hundred per cent safe.

Serenity Prayer

In the make-up room, a woman with hair dyed black and glossy as a crow pushed tan foundation into Carly's pores as if she was puttying a cracked wall. She had already whipped Carly's hair into a concoction the shape of a soft-serve ice-cream. Now she coloured Carly's eyebrows mahogany and her eyelids wine-grape purple.

'The studio lights bleach colours,' the woman had said. 'If I don't do this you'll look like a ghost.'

Carly closed her eyes as a tissue was pasted to her face. When the make-up woman peeled away the tissue, the imprint of a colourful clown came away with it.

'All done. Enjoy the show.'

She unclipped the napkin from Carly's neck and stood back, waiting with her hands on her hips, while Carly gathered her handbag and coat and tried to get up from the chair without seeing her gaudy make-up again in the mirror.

Next room down the hall was the Green Room.

It is exactly where she knows it will be. A table beside the door is loaded with plates of half-eaten crusty old sandwiches and limp slivers of canteloupe and honeydew melon. A grey-haired man sits in the far corner of the room tapping on a laptop. He is probably an actor or director Virginia worked with at the Queens Theatre.

'Hi,' Carly says, not too loudly, but loudly enough for an older man to hear.

He looks up.

'I was just going to introduce myself. I'm Virginia's sister. We might have met?'

'Virginia?' His fingers are still tracing along the trackpad as though his brain has gone on worrying at a problem while he gazes blankly at Carly. He could be a fixture of the room, an automaton. He'll be working at that computer into eternity as other guests come and go, as programs rise and fall in the ratings, as television itself disappears into electronic obscurity.

'Virginia Sherman. Who the show's about today.'

'No, I don't know her.' He returns his attention to the laptop.

The door swings open, knocking Carly further into the room.

'Jesus, sorry! Are you all right?' A young man presses his hands gently on different parts of her body as if he is checking for broken bones.

Without warning Carly wants to cry.

This is what she expected to happen. She would walk into a television studio and tell a funny story about her talented movie-star sister to a crowd of adoring fans. Next week this scene would be broadcast to a national audience in the millions. Carly's painted face, her cone hair, would be splashed across the nation while she relived the night-mare on the couch in her lounge room as the hard drive recorded her for posterity. She'd push aside the comforting arms of her husband and cry in jags and sob about having been born the dumpy, awkward sister, the plain one, the failure. This is what would happen when she stepped onto the stage of *This Is Your Life*. Her resentment, her jealousy, rolling across the screen for the entertainment of friends, enemies and strangers. What could be worse?

'Yes, I'm fine,' she told the young man, slipping back into her usual acquiescent self. 'Let's get this over with.'

'I'll take you to the side of the stage. You'll be able to hear yourself being introduced. Step onto the white marker tape at the edge of the stage and wait till your eyes adjust to the studio lights. Then you'll hear Mac ask you to come on stage. Someone will escort you to your seat.' He was saying all this as they wound their way through dark corridors that smelled like old cheese.

'I'll never find my way back,' she joked, but it wasn't a joke. She thought of poor lost Persephone. When she taught the Year Tens the Persephone story, one boy told her it was no big deal to live half the year in hell. 'We already do, miss,' he said. 'It's called school.'

The kind young man smiled. 'That's all right. I'll come and get you when you're done.' His hand touched Carly's elbow to prompt her each time they had to turn a corner. He had a downy blonde fuzz where he was probably trying to grow a beard, and his pants were too short. He was an innocent child guiding her into this dirty world of entertainment.

They pass through a section of the corridor where the lights have failed. The sudden darkness leaches sight from her eyes. Carly grasps the sleeve of the young man. He whispers to her to be brave, that if she can stay strong it will be over before she knows it. Endurance, that's all she needs – to play out every step until things reach their natural end. Carly isn't sure exactly what he's talking about.

They come into light again and she laughs with a sick feeling in her belly and she almost wants to turn back into the darkness.

'Endure,' he whispers again, pushing her in the small of the back with more force than she expected, propelling her forward.

They reach the maw of the stage. The boy nudges her forward a further few centimetres. 'Hang on till you hear yourself invited on stage. I'll be waiting back here when it's over.' He turns and sprints away down the passage, leaving her at the threshold.

When Carly told the other teachers she was doing this they interrogated her. 'Are you going to meet anyone famous besides your sister?' 'When will it be broadcast?' 'What will you wear?' They sent out sparks of excitement and anxiety and envy as if this was the most important thing that would ever happen to Carly, as if she was getting what everyone else wanted without having earned it. 'But you hardly ever watch TV!' one complained.

From the shadows at the side of the stage, the lights were so bright Carly couldn't see who was there. There was only an eye-stinging brilliance and the sound of many hands applauding. She stepped onto the white tape that marked the boundary between this world and the next. Her eyes closed involuntarily against the glare.

The boy had said Mac would introduce her. Who was Mac? The usual host was Roger Young. He would stand to the side at the beginning of the show, holding the big red book and reading out facts about the person's life so you could try to guess who it might be before the curtains swept open and the chosen person was revealed.

'And what did she say about this?' Carly heard a man say in a smooth caramel voice.

'She doesn't know,' Virginia answered.

'Well then,' the man who must be Mac said. 'Perhaps it's time she found out?'

For a stupid moment Carly wondered if the episode was about her and her life. A pathetic flare of ambition, like her colleagues had shown when they heard she'd be on TV. As if she'd had any kind of life worth talking about.

Her eyes are adjusting to the glare. An audience of women on raked seats faces the stage. A man sits high on the steps in the aisle between banks of audience members. He is holding a microphone and speaking toward the stage. He has a head of hair a woman would envy: thick, curly and golden. The hair of a god, or a luscious incubus. His face is familiar, soft-focus familiar, in the way photos of movie stars are familiar or like a story that you're telling someone but you trail off in confusion as you begin to wonder if it was a dream or a sitcom plot or if it actually happened.

All she needed to do was give the speech and sit down and smile. Perhaps kiss Virginia on the cheek and hug her the way they used to do when they met in public.

The stage was nothing more than the floor in front of the audience. Virginia, Carly's glamorous actress sister, sat in a chair beside Carly's husband, cradling his hand on her lap. No, cradling his hand *in* her lap and gazing into his face.

When she sees this, Carly's body is caught in a strange willy-willy. Her scalp stings as if her hair is being torn from her head. She retches. Something is scratching at her ankles — claws or thorns or unkempt fingernails. Then the willy-willy passes, leaving her uncannily calm.

Mac lounged on the steps between two banks of raked audience seats. He invited Carly to come in as if they were in his living room. Like a starstruck teenager she stepped into the light. A slant to the floor caused her to lurch and totter toward Glenn and Virginia. Her husband and her sister. She repeated it in her head. Husband and sister.

Glenn couldn't or wouldn't look in her direction. She had only seen him three hours ago, at breakfast this morning, where he was his usual surly morning self, grunting at the coffee maker and pulling on his suit jacket while he chewed at a piece of toast. How could he be here?

'Ladies and gentlemen, Mrs Carly Kantzakis,' Mac said, his voice rebounding from the studio's make-believe walls. 'Someone help the lady.'

Amid a cacophony of whistles and shouts and jeers from the audience, a man in a tight T-shirt bounced over to her and gripped her upper arm with his massive hand.

'This way, lady,' he muttered. He half lifted Carly to the podium, where an empty chair faced her sister and her husband.

She feels surprisingly flat. Perhaps it is shock. Perhaps you lose your sense of humiliation and rage under shockingly bright lights. She doesn't feel much at all, and that seems wrong. She crosses her legs, hears the rasp of stocking on stocking. Does it again the other way, hears it again. Time stops once more, a space of silence and stillness as she crosses and recrosses her legs in a queer seated dance. After a period that is nothing but the movement of her legs in their rhythmic nonsense scissoring, the sound comes back, distant at first – a crowd from afar, growing louder until she lifts her face and rage smashes up against her calm.

Mac leaned in. 'Carly, I think you've guessed what's going on here. How do you feel?'

The camera dolly trundled toward her. She wished she could wipe off the lurid painted face but it was too late for that. It was too late, wasn't it? Mac cleared his throat to get the attention of the crowd before he lifted the microphone to his lips.

'Carly, do you have anything to say to your sister? Your husband?'

She raised her head. Why would they do this? Was Virginia broke again? Stupid alcoholic Glenn had no idea what he was getting into. Carly had lived with Princess Virginia and her neediness all her life.

The calls from the studio audience were gathering like a rehearsed chorus into a chant and accompanying clap.

'Car-ly. Car-ly. Car-ly.'

It makes her smile. As if she is the famous sister, the one loved by the tabloids. Is this how it feels to be golden? People calling to her. Her name turned into a song. Everyone wanting her yet knowing hardly anything about her. Mac smiles as if he has heard her thoughts. She turns her face away, blushing. When she glances back he is still smiling at her. Space and time are curving around her body, tucking her into a tight uncomfortable fold as Mac reads her mind and keeps smiling.

Carly could see the iris of the camera opening. She knew the kind of thing they were hoping she'd say, the weeping and shrieking they wanted her to do. She had grown up with television and its conventions. She had laughed at the women on shows like this who lunged at their husbands, tried to tear their hair out, who moaned and wept, who bared themselves.

But Carly didn't want to be one of those women. She was here on stage, betrayed, sure enough, but by a man she had already grown to despise. Sitting there, watched by a crowd of screamers, she could only come up with this one thought. The words popped out of her mouth, harmless missiles out of a peashooter. 'Why didn't I leave you years ago?'

A small man holding up a large placard raced backward and forward across the studio floor in front of the audience. The placard said *Laugh*. Scattered on the floor at the side of the stage were more that said *Scream* and *Howl* and *Hiss* and other instructions for whatever he wanted the audience to do. Right now they were doing it all at once. A woman in clingy aqua pants barrelled down the stairs, arms flailing, calling out that Carly should punch the dirty bastard. She was caught at the bottom of the steps by two hefty men and escorted backstage to the cheering of the crowd.

Mac stood. He tamped down the noise with hand gestures until there were only a few catcalls coming from the back rows.

'Glenn? Would I be wrong to say your wife doesn't seem as surprised as you expected?'

Glenn's lip curled in that special way that Carly used to find sexy. 'Don't believe that shit. She's surprised all right. This is her fake "I don't give a damn" routine. The one I've put up with for nine years.'

'Hey!' an angry voice shouted down from the top tier of the seats. A slim woman in jeans and a T-shirt with her hair in two girlish pigtails sprang out of her seat. 'You didn't like your wife? Why'd you stay? Why didn't you run off with the famous sister instead of humiliating this woman here on TV?'

As the crowd applauded, Glenn looked off to the side. He sighed, the way he did with Carly when he had no answer to a question and he wanted to pretend the question was stupid to begin with. But the woman wasn't having any of that. She pushed aside the blonde next to her and clambered across three more people to reach the aisle, where she put her hands on her hips and her lips to the microphone that a stagehand had raced up the stairs to hold in front of her face.

'You answer me, mister. Why are you doing this?'

Virginia lifted the stage microphone and murmured into it. 'It's not his fault. We fell in love. We didn't know how to tell her.'

'You shut up, you washed-up hack!'

Virginia shook her head, lip trembling, features emulsified into the vulnerable haunted face that got her into movies in the first place.

Pigtail woman jabbed her scarlet-nailed finger at Virginia. 'A slut like you took my husband away too but at least she didn't go on national television to tell me.'

Carly starts when she hears that line. 'A slut like you took my husband away but at least she didn't go on national television to tell me.' The line is thrumming through her. She's heard it so many times before, but where?

'Steady, ladies,' Mac interrupted. He'd been moving around the studio, and now he came to rest behind Virginia, placing a hand on her shoulder as he spoke. 'Virginia, what do you need to say to Carly?'

'No, stop.' Carly surged out of her seat, tugged down the back of her dress. 'I'm not going on with this. I won't give permission for this to be broadcast.' She'd received the contract in the mail, seen her sister's name as the feature of the show, glanced at the clauses on the first page about network serial repeat rights and other TV jargon, and signed it without looking any further.

Placard man scooted up and down in front of the audience rows again. The shiny eager faces responded with boos and hisses and foot stamping.

'Forget it.' Carly turned to the rows of angry faces. 'I'm not going to be your freak show. Find someone else.'

Behind her Mac spoke to the audience in a conspiratorial whisper. 'Ladies, don't you find it amazing that no one, absolutely no one, reads the fine print of contracts. I would have thought our Carly here, a teacher of all things, would have read what she was getting herself into.'

'So sue me.' There was nothing to stop her leaving.

Or so she thinks, but when she wheels around and strides to the stage entrance she finds two T-shirted brutes standing with their arms crossed in front of the open door.

'Get out of the way.'

They remain motionless. Carly pushes her arm between them and tries to shove her shoulder through, the way you would at a gate that won't open properly. The men don't budge. They're welded together like the two-headed dog guarding the gates of hell. So it is true. She is in hell. Why? Why is this happening to her?

The crowd was screaming, laughing, hooting. Rage percolated in Carly's gut. She muttered threats at the guardians about assault charges, keeping her voice down and her back to the cameras. She found herself hissing at them like a cat. 'I will not let this happen. I will not accept this.'

'My, my.' Mac had climbed the audience steps again and was looking down. 'Carly seems to have found her inner fury. So Glenn, I guess this isn't the ice queen you were telling us about.'

'Stop filming me!' Carly shouted, still facing away from the crowd and the cameras and Mac. 'I refuse to allow this.'

She certainly couldn't look at Virginia and Glenn. Glenn, who had been telling this mad chorus that she was an ice queen. Glenn, who chewed nicotine gum sixteen hours a day. Glenn, who had a swatch of wiry ginger hair at the base of his spine that she could no longer bear to touch. Glenn, who had lusted after her sister from the moment he saw her. Her sister – spendthrift, actress, star, family favourite. Selfish witch. They deserved each other but Carly would not say it aloud, because she was on TV. She was on her way to becoming an ugly reality star, and she'd watched enough TV and read enough magazines to know what that meant: if she allowed the invective to flow, the couple would be recast as the good guys, leaving her the ranting bitter cause of their coming together. She would not give them the satisfaction. She would not give them the airtime, the gloating, the happiness they thought this alliance might provide them. Shame had filled her, shame and rage and a new iron stubbornness. She would not endure this humiliation.

The cameras on their dollies wheeled around the studio floor trying to capture her face in all its mortification while she sidled to a corner and faced the wall like a naughty child at school.

'I have to say, ladies, this is not great television.' Mac sighed. 'What can we do to bring Carly out of her shell? Hmm?'

The chant started up again.

'Car-ly. Car-ly. Car-ly.'

'Tell those bastards what you think, Carly! We're on your side,' one woman screamed.

No one was on Carly's side. That, at least, was clear.

'Go on, Carly!'

'Smack that bitch, Carly!'

'Car-ly. Car-ly. Car-ly. Car-ly. Car-ly.'

They think they can unleash her rage. They are wrong. How strange her name sounds when it becomes a chant from the audience. It could be someone else's name. Car-ly. Ka-li, she realises. Kali. Religions of the world, Year Eight. Kali, the goddess of destruction and change. Can you destroy by doing nothing? Can you banish by not accepting?

She remained perfectly still in her corner, refusing to turn around. As long as she didn't participate there was no show.

The shouting from the crowd slowly died down. The audience members began to chat among themselves. Mac raced down the stairs and murmured over her shoulder, promised her a chance to respond with dignity.

She ignored him and waited. The warm-up comedian faced down the mutinous audience, cajoled them into a few laughs, ran out of material. Mac, leaning over her shoulder and speaking so close to her face that his breath heated her cheek, threatened her with lawsuits. She waited.

The show's producer hurried onto the stage. He rode the other shoulder, his muttering a spray of warm spit. Time passed and her legs ached with tension and she needed to go to the toilet but she closed her eyes, her ears, her mind, and waited.

The stage manager ordered the operators to shut down the cameras. The big lights went off with a clank. She waited.

People chattered as they edged across the rows. She heard the rumble and clatter as they filed down the staircase and out through the exit. One or two called out to her. 'Goodbye, Carly!' 'Good luck, Carly. Stick it to him!'

After a long time in the dark of the shut-down stage, she felt someone behind her. A warm presence, a scent of pine. A hand touched her arm. Her body had tipped forward with the rigidity of a board leaning against a wall. Her forehead pressed against the flimsy studio partition. She stared at her feet, knotted that morning, an aeon ago, a minute ago, into the straps of her best silver high heels. She remembered that time she woke from a dream in which actors from her favourite TV drama were carrying her in an open coffin.

'You can turn around now.' The young man who had led her to this place stood with his hand out to take hers. 'They've shut down the cameras. The audience is gone.'

'Is it over?' she asked.

'I'm afraid not,' he said. 'Let's go.'

Everything had fizzled and left an eerie dim silence, an electric loneliness, like the empty drawn-out moment when the TV is turned off.

She takes hold of his forearm and follows him out to the corridor, weak and prickly with the leftover adrenaline of her emotional storm. All she wants to do is go home, lie down, take a few days off work. It has been hellish, unbelievable really, but she stood her ground. She would not talk this through with those betrayers, not on reality TV, not in her home, not anywhere. Never.

All she wants to do is sleep. So tired she is dizzy. Things have taken on a dreamy quality. Is she asleep, dreaming? There is tiredness, yes, but there's more. A kind of echo of time passing, or moving. A swirling, eddying sense of the movement of time.

Back in the make-up room, the woman was waiting for Carly. She held a sponge already loaded with tan foundation. Carly sat down in the chair. The make-up woman looked familiar. She was probably one of the parents Carly had talked with at some parent–teacher day.

The woman stroked the first bars of tan colour onto Carly's white skin.

'The studio lights are hell,' she said. 'They bleach out colours. If I don't do this …'

Caramels

Across the creek a couple is squatting on the muddy bank, shoes and socks in a pile behind them on the grass, pants rolled up to their knees like little kids at the playground, except they're no kids they're pushing at least sixty both of them. The bloke is tying the string around a knob of reeking meat I can smell from here, green meat rotten enough to tickle the senses of the yabbies below, those innocent crusties hiding in their lairs harming no one when down through the water comes an alluring gob of steak.

Makes me realise I'm a little hungry myself.

She's giggling and peering at him dipping the temptation into the water, probably can't even see the string without her reading glasses, skinny grey stripe at her scalp like some tribal decoration except she'll dye it away tomorrow pretending she's ten years younger and she'll have a glass of dry white wine with a bocconcini and tomato and basil pizza and we'll all be lovely darling darling.

A bocconcini pizza would suit me fine right now, the trouble with this reserve being no one eats dinner here, after all who'd bother carting across their pizza or fish and chips and a can of Coke just to abandon it half eaten in the dark for a kiss with the girlfriend when they can parbloodytake at a restaurant up in Lygon St, everything provided, eat and drink your fill then go for a lovely walk along the Merri Creek and make Merri.

Bugger, they've got one.

Poor little yabbie, tasty morsel of rotten meat dangling in front of the house, you peek out lured by that irresistible smell, you take the lump in one claw and it is so damn good you can't let go even though the bastards upstairs are reeling you in and you know that disaster's waiting for you but something inside has locked on to that smell and you find yourself clinging on as you're pulled up through the water, gentle as a flower drifting in a stream, the light getting lighter until it hurts your little stalky eyes and you know you should let go, you know it's all over for you if you don't but that smell has reached into you, taken hold of your mind, you've damn well cleaved to that delicious smell and it will be the death of you.

And when you break the water there they are, the bastards staring at you and exclaiming to each other what a beauty you are, and you are a beauty, you're a hulk, Godzilla of the yabbie world and still you can't let go, you're frozen in your death wish and they drop you and your meat, that useless little dreg of Judas meat, into a bucket of clean fresh water that makes you want to gag and that's it, the shock wakes you up and you think Jesus what the hell have I done

161

and now, you idiot, you epicurean fool, you start trying to escape, your claws scrabbling against the smooth blue bucket walls but you're done for.

There it goes splash, one later to be served up on a bed of seduction salad with a chardonnay jus and a side of I love you I really do now roll over darling he'll say to the ancient scraggy lovebird who's cooing and snorking over catching a yabbie like it's fishery foreplay, look at me you juicy morsel I'm a big brave fishing man at the creek.

Me and my one-on-one love life on the other hand excuse my pun prefer a bit of privacy, which is more than most you'd guess from the shenanigans going on late at night in this reserve that I like to call the Merri motel, frequented by your underage snoggers and the ones who've left their wedding rings in the glove box for a sashay in the weedy dark with some lucky lady.

Sadly no woman would look at me now with my particularly dreddy hairstyle du jour that I can't wash since the drought and those cheapskates stealing water for their carnations so the council takes the heads off all the garden taps in the parks, and believe you me I'm not putting my head in a basin at the public toilet with half your ablution-ists so blind drunk they think the sink's the dunny or the vomitorium, can't tell you how many coiled-up turds I've found in the sink and I look at the abominations and realise those idiots must have climbed up and squatted like storks to do a shit in there. Amazing what a bottle of sauvignon blanc will achieve for the human body.

Oh hell, here it comes.

If it isn't the social worker bastard come to gooey all over me, Max have you taken your medication, Max are you eating anything, Max do you want a place to sleep tonight, I tell him you twit, social workers are supposed to be girls, you're a greasy old bastard from Footscray, why don't you get a proper job and stop hassling decent citizens like myself, and he always says shut up Max if you had any sense at all you'd be living in the Housing Commission with a cleaner you moron.

I like the fresh air, haven't I told you that five hundred times I tell him and he always says there's no fresh air around you Max, you stink like something died in your pocket and I tell him it did, it's my self-respect, and he says take your hand off it Max, you could walk out of this today and get a job in an engineering firm and I tell him that's what put me here in the first place remember.

Today he hands me a plastic bag saying I've brought you a few things like a toothbrush and toothpaste because Max your breath would melt the duco off a car.

So that's what happened in the carpark the other day I say, I thought it was the hot wind.

I like that the old Footscray do-gooder sometimes brings me a feed.

We sit on the high bank and open up the paper and I've got to say the aroma of fish and chips is like rotten meat to a yabbie, I can't resist it, hungry as anything and him telling me he got a piece of flake and three potato cakes and chips, so I ask what are you going to eat and whammo he pulls out another package from his social worker man bag saying here's mine and handing me a can of beer and this is it, this is a life good enough for any old bastard, the sun shining, a pair of lovebirds torturing yabbies across the creek and a lapful of fatty batter and salt making my head spin and my mouth fill up with saliva that I wash down with a mouthful of beer.

To hell with the toothbrush and toothpaste, it would probably knock out the last of my teeth anyway.

See them over there I say to him and he looks at the squidgy love seniors dangling their meat in the creek, they're flouting the laws of the reserve I tell him, you should arrest them, they're stealing the fauna, and they're going to cook it up in white wine and extra virgin olive oil and boast about it like it's a prize marlin they've wrestled with for hours, man against nature, those bastards are turning my reserve into a dinner party.

Max he says, stop looking at them or they'll spot you for the perv you are.

Mate, sitting next to you I'm suddenly the dapper gentleman I tell him, look at yourself you've got to get rid of that fungus growing on your chin, what is that some kind of fashion statement or you forgot to spray on the Exit Mould this morning.

It drives the ladies wild he tells me and he gives it a quick fondle like he's Rodin's thinker and I tell him that oil off your hot chips will give it extra shine and special aroma and he says yep that's it, hot chip oil is irresistible to the kind of lady I'm looking for. Anyway Max your wife wants to see you.

They've caught another yabbie, splash into the bucket for the doomed clacker and they're probably already planning the four-course dinner yabbie à la puy lentil ragout with a twist of smug satisfaction, we caught these ourselves didn't we darling, clink go the shiraz boys clink clink clink.

Max?

Fish and chips here in my lap like a piece of stinking irresistible meat and Mr Social Worker's scratching at his weedface and looking all dewy-eyed at the beautiful nature around us, we're having a lovely picnic aren't we. Sure we are you traitor.

So whaddya reckon Max he says, I could get you a shower at the Brotherhood, give you a couple of bucks for a coffee.

Not having eaten a big meal in one go like this for a while I'll probably end up in the vomitorium tonight fighting the drunks and junkies for a bowl of my own.

I don't need a wash I tell him, the joy of the outdoor life is freedom to smell like a walking corpse, no wait, it's freedom to be a walking corpse so bugger off and let me live my wonderful life okay.

Big fisherman and his missus across the creek are packing up their Ikea fishing stools and burbling over their dinner in a bucket and I see the bloke's pretending to help her up while he cops a feel of her arse with his big pincer.

So Max?

Don't say anything to me not a word I tell the social worker bastard, because nothing you say can be right and you're in my domain here I left them everything.

I'm not saying anything he says, except kids, I'll just say that one word kids and leave it with you Max.

Where's my dessert I say, you can't treat a man to a meal without dessert, you'll never get me into bed this way and he nods and pulls out a packet of caramels.

Shit I say, did she tell you about the caramels and he says yeah she said to bring a packet of caramels and tell you Emily's in high school now and she needs help with maths, I promised I'd do it, it's done, okay now let's eat our chips Max, I don't want to mess with you.

Mr and Mrs Ikea are off now, they look back and wave at us for the dinner party tonight when they can say we saw a homeless man poor old thing, we couldn't have caught the yabbies without him, it was his stench that brought them scooting out of the water, titter titter ooh we shouldn't talk like that.

I'm performing a social service I tell the Footscray bastard, entertainment at the Merri motel they should be paying me.

You're keeping the area clear of perverts too he says, the ones with a sense of smell anyway.

I tell the Footscray social worker hey I saw your ex outside the supermarket with her new loverman and they gave me a fiver, but maybe I shouldn't have said it,

Footscray's an okay bloke even if he is a do-gooder with a face like a hairy arse.

Sorry, your kids how are they I say and I think I'm being charming hobo master of the Merri manor but the hairy-arse face folds up like a squashed bun and he says they're settling into the new house and new stepfather and all that, it's okay, he'll be seeing them soon and master of the Merri misstep me backs off with a mighty flourish of a fart, sorry mate I say, too much gourmet food in the middle of the day.

I'll be off now the Footscray hairy arse says, you take care of yourself Max.

I will I tell him, sorry about your kids.

You should take me up on the offer of a shower he says, the park ranger'll be onto you for suffocating the native animals.

I'll think about it I say, maybe next year.

I'm not taking the caramels he says when he's halfway up the bank, his big hairy arse, the real one, squeezed in his pants with the effort of getting up the hill, I'll leave them with you Max.

They're tasty I call back, too rich for me these days.

I'll leave them with you he says again, you might change your mind, and the last I see of him is two big arse cheeks disappearing over the ridge.

This is the best time of day at the Merri motel.

The picnickers have gone home and the rooters and ranters have yet to arrive, the birds are starting their dusk calls, the council cleaner's been through the dunnies, the council gardener's lunch leftovers are in the bin, the free newspapers are lying around on park benches.

The yabbies, or what's left of them, slumber at peace in their dark quiet caves under the water.

Something to Take Care Of

The girl balances on the top rail of the round yard, her heels knocking against the middle rail, one-two, one-two. Inside the ring, her grandfather steps closer to the chestnut filly. The horse is part Arab with a fine narrow head and a short straight back. The end of the lead rope dangles from the grandfather's left hand. He stretches his right hand toward the filly but in the distance a chainsaw starts up and she startles and breaks into a canter around the outer rim of the round yard. Her hooves hitting the sand sound like the thud of doors shutting in the distance.

'It's okay,' he murmurs to the filly. 'It's okay, lovely girl, don't worry, it's okay.'

Joe, the girl's stepfather, stands in a larger square yard that encloses the round yard.

'Can you see her tail, Holly?' he says. 'See how she holds it up when she gallops? That's the Arab in her.'

Beside Joe is a second small pony that will eventually be his ride. The stocky dun gelding with a cropped mohawk mane throws his head up and down as the Arab heaves out a great snort before slowing to a trot, then a walk.

Joe rests his hand on the dun pony's neck. When he and the grandfather went to buy the horses, cheap because no one had ridden them for a year, the filly was the wilder of the two. She had been broken in and never ridden again. 'We'll settle her down,' the grandfather had said at the exact moment she swung her head around to nip at the man who was tapping her rump with a stick to move her forward. Joe cracked out a nervous laugh. But Holly was begging for a pony of her own, and it would be a distraction. They could do it together with the grandfather's guidance. Learn to ride. Take on the responsibility of looking after an animal.

The grandfather had instructed him and the girl in some basics before the horses arrived. Never stand behind a horse, never stand directly in front of a horse, keep a hand on the horse at all times to let it know you're there, always speak gently. Then Joe had spent hours and hours on the internet watching videos of horse-training. Nothing had prepared him for these warm-blooded wilful animals with ears that seemed to have their own semaphore language.

Now the three humans and two horses have passed four days together. Joe has groomed the pony each day, brushing the mud and dust from its shaggy coat and slowly untangling its tail. He has learned how to lift its hooves one by one to check for stones, how to fit a halter and how to hold the rope correctly. He has walked it around the agist-ment property ten times, watching other owners handle their horses, and then he has come back to learn more from the grandfather working with the Arab in the round yard.

'Holly, look,' Joe says. 'Look over here.' Holly turns, and as he says to the pony, 'We're good buddies now, right?' he reaches under its chin and tickles the long hairs to make the pony toss its head as if saying yes. Holly giggles.

Joe's hands are always busy. Although his jeans are held up by a belt, the weakness in his left hip means they slide down and he must hitch them up every once in a while.

He tugs on the halter rope. The pony resists, bracing itself on the sandy surface so that its weight cannot be shifted.

'I can't move this stubborn mule again,' Joe says to the grandfather.

'Remember? Walk past his shoulder, catch his eye, then turn and walk away and he'll follow you. Don't look back.'

The grandfather has done the same thing with the Arab. She stands close behind him, her head at his shoulder, her warm breath fanning his ear, and he reaches up around her neck and plays with her mane, moving his hand up the arch to the poll to massage the tendon underneath. As the Arab dips her head he presses his cheek against hers, still scratching the top of her neck.

'That's my girl. That's the way.'

'When can I ride her?' the girl asks. 'Today?' She is like her mother. Driven mad by waiting.

'It won't be too long. She's a fine little filly, she just needs some love, time and love.'

'What about Bobby?'

'I thought you wanted to change Bobby's name. Didn't you say it wasn't a good name for a horse?'

Joe is leading Bobby past the girl now. The pony plods with an even gait but Joe drags his left leg and when he turns he has to heft his body in a stiff action instead of swivelling on a heel or a toe. Before Holly's mother left she had started needling him about his limp. *Hurry up, you useless cripple.*

Holly swings her legs over the rail and jumps to the ground. Bobby curls his neck to look at her with interest.

'Can I pat him?'

'Of course you can. He's our horse now.'

She is ten years old. Even though it is school holidays she wears jeans, grubby runners and a red school jumper with the crest embroidered on the chest. Her blonde hair twists over her shoulders in scarecrow pigtails. When she reaches for Bobby's muzzle he tosses his head again, startling her. She retreats, looking to Joe. Even before her mother left she had trusted his word first.

'It's all right,' Joe says. 'Make sure he can see you properly. Stand to the side of his head.'

Holly inches forward, head high to conceal her nervousness, and strokes the pony's thick muscular neck.

'Good girl. This old fella won't hurt you.'

In the round yard the grandfather is running his hands over the Arab, along her flank, over her withers, up and down her legs and under her belly, all the while talking quietly to her. She steps lightly around him but doesn't baulk. He's an old man and although he has no fear it's fifty years since he worked a horse. His own father was a jockey, an old-school type who flogged the horses when they disobeyed or ran too slow. The grandfather learned a different way to handle horses from a strapper girl he would have married if she hadn't run off with a track rider from another stable. She taught him how to train a horse with attention and patience. *They're talking to us in their own language*, she used to tell him. *You have to learn how to hear what they say.* The horse's muscles rippling under his hands, the petal-soft muzzle, the rich smell of horseshit baking in the sun, the snorts and whinnies of the other horses agisted in the paddocks nearby bring back such memories of that stable girl he can feel the grip on his heart that he used to get when he heard her voice ringing from the stalls.

'Granddad, why do they call it breaking a horse?'

'Because that's what they used to do. That's what they did with this girl. They beat her around the ears. See?' His hand slides up the neck of the filly and fondles her left ear. She shies away, puffing and rolling her eyes. He goes back to the steady reassuring strokes along her flank, rubbing her shoulder deeply, pushing the skin back and forth across the muscles. He's tired already but he doesn't want Joe and Holly to see. In an hour the light will be gone and he can go home and sit in front of the fire and think about the stable girl, her smell of straw and sweat.

'That filly is so much better already,' Joe remarks.

'Maybe it's time we put the bridle on Bobby, see how he takes the bit,' the grandfather says. 'Bring him back in here.'

Holly unlatches the gate. Joe catches Bobby's eye then walks away with the rope slung loosely from his left hand. Bobby follows him into the ring.

'He's not going to like it,' the grandfather says. He has unclipped the lead rope from the Arab's halter but she stays beside him, alert, watching Joe and Bobby approach. He nods at Holly to latch the gate behind them.

'Can I call her Princess?' the girl asks.

'She already has a name, darling. She's Redling Dana, remember?' It's Joe who answers, although she could have been asking either of them. She doesn't call him Dad because he's not the dad she knew for the first six years of her life. She doesn't call him Joe because when he first moved in it didn't seem right. It went on like that for so long, her not knowing what to call him, that it became natural for her not to call him anything. When she wants his attention she goes to him, touches his arm or gets right up to his face to speak.

'Can I call her Princess Redling Dana?'

Neither of the men answers. The grandfather has fetched the bridle from the bucket of horse tack sitting outside the round-yard rail. He turns his back to Bobby and Joe as he untangles the leather straps.

'I'm going to put the bridle on him,' he tells Joe, hiding it behind him as he approaches Bobby. 'Hold the pony steady, there, high on the rope. And pat him, reassure him.'

Joe takes hold of the pony's halter under its chin while the grandfather drapes his arm across the pony's poll. Bobby is tense. They wait, Joe stroking his flank, the grandfather resting his arm over the poll. After a couple of minutes, Bobby relaxes. His head drops. The grandfather eases the bit between his lips and against his big yellow teeth and pushes his thumb into Bobby's mouth. Bobby won't open.

'He doesn't like it,' Holly calls from the top rail where she has climbed up again to watch. She shades her eyes. The sun has come out again, although it is chilly, and the breeze cuts into their cotton clothes. Thin clouds are flowing across the sky like spills of pale milk.

'No, he doesn't like it much. We'll be patient.' The grandfather is breathing heavily as he wiggles his thumb into Bobby's mouth to persuade Bobby to open. 'Keep him steady, Joe, I don't want to lose my thumb.'

After a minute Bobby can't sustain his resistance. His teeth part. The grandfather slips the bit into Bobby's mouth, over his meaty tongue, eases the bridle up over his ears and the deed is done. Bobby doesn't like it but he can't get it out. He chews at the bit and rolls his tongue up over the metal pieces and then under them. The bit clanks against his teeth.

'It's too loose,' the grandfather says as he slides the halter out from under the bridle. 'We'll tighten it tomorrow. He'll be used to it in no time.'

'So should I try riding him?' Joe asks. He is tired too. He's resting the weight on his strong leg, but he can keep going until the dark comes. They're making good progress.

'Why not?' The grandfather backs up against the rail to give Joe more room. The filly is beside him, nosing the pocket of his jacket.

Joe knows from watching other people working horses at the agistment property over the last four days that he has to mount quickly and not let Bobby take control.

'Do you think you should do it?' he asks the grandfather, who shakes his head and smiles. If he got up on a horse he wouldn't be able to walk tomorrow.

Holly is watching closely. Joe gives her the thumbs up and hauls himself onto the pony. Bobby is so surprised that for a moment he stands still. Then he takes off at a fast trot, heading to the rail to try to dislodge his rider.

'Pull the right rein hard,' the grandfather calls, 'hard! Hold it up against your belly. Push your weight to the ground!'

Joe drags at Bobby's mouth to force him away from the rail. Already he's sliding on the horse's back. As Bobby turns and his jerky trotting eases, Joe slips sideways and backward until, in an unplanned manoeuvre, he lets go of the reins, pushes off Bobby and miraculously lands on his feet behind the pony. Bobby trots to the opposite end of the round yard and stretches his head through the rails, straining for the grass growing on the other side.

'That might be enough for Bobby for today,' the grandfather says. 'Unless you want to try again?'

'Not really.' Joe laughs. He doesn't look at Holly, who has her legs wrapped around the rail and is hanging sideways to pat Bobby's haunch. His hip is aching now. He looks at the sky, sees with relief the luminescence of the clouds fading to a sheety grey.

The grandfather turns his attention back to the Arab.

'Let's get you moving, beautiful lady.'

After Joe has caught Bobby's reins and led him to the outer enclosure, the grandfather steps away from the filly and claps his hands twice. She kicks up and canters the length of the rail. He walks in a tight circle in the middle of the ring, staying just behind her direct line of vision so that she keeps moving. When she has been lunging for a couple of minutes, he stops and turns away from her. She slackens her pace and finally comes to rest, watching him. He moves to her, slowly, lifts his hand and strokes her long narrow nose.

'You're a good girl. You're settling down now, aren't you? You're going to be just fine.'

'I had a thought,' Joe says from the outer enclosure where he and Bobby have been idling. 'Jumping on didn't work, so what if I put some weight on Bobby, like we saw that woman do yesterday with the wild pony?'

'You could try it.' The grandfather looks at his watch. Half an hour of daylight left.

Holly has climbed down off the rail and is rummaging through the pile of horse blankets next to the bucket of gear. She chooses one to draw over her shoulders.

'Look, I'm a horse.' She mock canters around the outside of the rail, the checked blanket flaring behind her. 'What are we having for tea tonight?'

In the far corner of the yard, Joe stretches his arms and then his torso cautiously across where the saddle would sit on Bobby's back. He gradually lowers his weight onto the pony. His feet are on the ground, but the rest of him is hanging over the horse like a corpse. Bobby starts moving and Joe tiptoes alongside to keep his balance, still draped over Bobby's back.

'This seems to be working,' Joe calls, his voice muffled from speaking upside down into the pony's flank.

'Can we have fish and chips?' Holly asks.

Bobby doesn't seem to notice as Joe pushes himself further and further across the horse's back until he can swing his leg over and they are once again horse and rider. Joe's long legs hang either side of Bobby's round belly. He holds the reins loosely. They walk the perimeter of the square yard and when they reach their original starting point Joe slides off and pats Bobby on the shoulder.

'We might get Chinese takeaway. Something with vegetables.'

'So is he okay to ride now?' Holly asks. Even though she is still wearing the horse rug, she's shivering. She drags her feet as she walks backward around the ring, shoes making furrows in the sand.

A mist is beginning to form on the fields, blurring the edges of fences and trees in the distance.

'He'll be ready soon,' Joe says. 'He's a good pony. He knows what he has to do.'

The grandfather opens the gate of the round yard and urges the Arab out into the larger enclosure. She can sense freedom. Her tail is high as she trots around, tossing her head and kicking up her heels. She calls out to the other horses and a couple answer.

'We'll collect the gear and take the ponies back to their paddock now, I think. It's been a good day.'

The darkness is coming fast. Joe collects the rugs and drapes them over the rail, ready to clip onto the horses for the cold night ahead. He loops Bobby's reins around the middle rail. The grandfather sorts the tack. They'll take off the bridle and halter after they've led the ponies through the three gates to their own paddock.

'Holly, do you want to help me put the rug on Bobby?' Joe asks.

'Oh,' Holly says, 'I thought ...'

Her tone of voice makes them both turn in time to see the Arab trot through the gate Holly has opened into the paddock beyond. When the filly sees the open space in front of her, she breaks into a gallop. Two other horses in the paddock catch her excitement. The two men and the girl watch in the thickening mist as the three horses race away in a wide arc. They disappear from view, with only the sound of their hooves on the earth giving any hint of their existence, and then they reappear on the opposite side of the long paddock, dancing and snorting hot steam.

'Oh God, we'll never get her back.' Joe covers his eyes with his hand. Holly takes his other hand in hers.

'I'm sorry. I'm really sorry.'

As if she has heard, the Arab trots across the paddock toward them.

'Come on, girl, come to me, come on.' The grandfather's voice is calm, steady. He holds the lead rope ready to clip to her halter. It seems as though the Arab is listening. She moves hesitantly in their direction, dipping her head, until at the last moment she hears the whinny of another horse and she is gone, galloping the length of the paddock.

'I'm sorry, Granddad.' Holly's voice wavers. Joe puts his arm around her and murmurs consolingly.

'Don't worry, darling. It's okay. I guess we can leave her in this paddock tonight and explain to the people tomorrow when we come back and move her.'

The grandfather knows they can't leave her there overnight. A stallion and a gelding agist in the paddock. A new filly will upset the dynamic, create a dangerous situation. A fight could break out. Valuable horses could be injured. He pats Holly on the head.

'It'll be all right. She'll come to me. She'll come back.'

Joe doesn't believe him. He goes back to fixing the rug on Bobby, encouraging Holly to duck under the pony's neck and buckle the front strap against his big chest. He thinks about buying beef and vegetables in black bean sauce for tea, or sweet and sour fish. Or maybe a chicken and a salad. He tries to keep his mind off the mother who still emails him, although he'd never tell Holly or the grandfather. She addresses him as *Dear Crip*, and accuses him of stealing her family. Her rambling emails taunt him for being soft and a loser and she demands he send her money, but he's stopped doing that.

Bobby waits at the rail, ready to be led to his paddock. Holly leans in close to feel his warmth.

The grandfather, exhausted, walks away into the misty green paddock filled with the shapes of horses, the lead rope trailing behind him like a slow-burning fuse.

Territory

Friday evenings we gathered before dark in the cafe. In March the twilight came at about seven thirty, with the heat from meats and pasta and sauces already steaming up the cafe windows. The dusky neon and streetlights made the glass light up like cinema screens. People passing by could have been actors, extras in a movie, seen through a mist, a window in Paris, the curtain of a noodle bar in a futuristic Los Angeles.

It had been two months already. Emma and Shannon and I were the only ones who never missed a Friday, and we were always the first to arrive. I ordered a martini, 'Because I like a bit of spirit.' That was the line, the ritual to set the mood. I would sit on that martini till nine, when we set out. Emma and Shannon preferred wine. They were served by a new waiter who smiled shyly, glancing at Shannon as he poured her twice the normal amount.

'What about me?' Emma complained. The waiter blushed and topped up her glass before hurrying back to the kitchen.

The cafe was kitted out in rough-hewn wooden chairs and tables and the floor was polished concrete, which meant the wine was twelve dollars a glass instead of seven. Moisture condensing on the windows formed tiny rivulets that had seeped into the timber sill and caused the varnish to blister and crack. I found myself picking at the crisp flakes of varnish as we waited, the same way I used to pick at sunburn and scabs, feeling the creepy satisfaction of the dead parts of my body peeling away and leaving that pink baby skin, all soft and new and yet scarred at the same time.

Each time someone entered the cafe, their presence was announced by the squeak or rap of shoes on that concrete and the shift in the air: everything in the cafe was brittle and there was nothing to absorb sound or sensation except our human bodies. Perhaps that added to the jittery excitement that built as we sipped our drinks, waiting to see who would arrive, and what they would be wearing. At nine o'clock, six of us were sitting together, ready.

By the time we stepped outside, the night had sharpened into hard-edged shadows under a full moon and a clear sky. Emma hugged herself.

'I should have brought a coat.'

She wore the dress we had seen in the Dangerfield window. It was a sack, shapeless and khaki-coloured with massive pockets sewn on the outside and a ragged hem. Urban guerilla girl chic, the shop assistant called it. 'You should wear bright stripy tights or knee socks with it,' she said. 'And platform shoes. Maybe even a bow in your hair, *Alice in Wonderland* style.' That's exactly what Emma had done. She looked crazy, dangerous, fun.

Shannon was in pink. She played demure better than the rest of us. Pressed jeans, a relaxed pink T-shirt, darker pink cardigan. Her auburn hair brushed straight, thick and soft over her shoulders. A clean face with a hint of blusher. Bree had gone moody and Goth with black clothes and dark wine lipstick, and Ozlem was the opposite, all frothy in light-coloured flounces and ribbons. Lu had chosen the shiny disco look. I wore my usual: black skirt above the knees, tight fluffy blue jumper cropped at the waist, black leggings, low heels, hair in a bun.

That was the only thing you might question about us. Other girls who went out in a group looked more alike. Arty types with arty types; girls who knew how to pick up wearing the uniform of short hip-hugging skirt, skyscraper heels, mascara and lipstick; anxious country girls in a giggly bunch trying too hard with their top buttons undone but their jeans too loose and complexions that sang of fresh air and cream. We were a mixed-up crowd, sometimes mistaken as a hens' night or a victorious hockey club, out on one of those occasions when different kinds of girls come together to celebrate.

'Did you hear Suze got into medicine?' Shannon asked as we linked arms in the street. 'They gave her a supplementary exam.'

'I always knew she would.'

In our final year of high school Suze and I sat beside each other in biology. I'd lean over and copy whatever she was writing because she understood it in a way no one else in class did, as if she were a witchdoctor reading entrails. On a diagram where I'd see blue and pink splotches and dense topographic maps, she would see the anterior vena cava, an aberrant squamous cell, the deep mysterious structure of living things. The shimmying fishtails under the microscope spoke to her in ways I couldn't fathom, even with the study notes at my elbow. I knew she would end up studying the human body.

Emma had said she'd like to try the Kale Bar, so we tripped along the footpath talking about our studies and jobs, parting like a flock of birds to allow other pedestrians through and re-forming to take up other conversations, other chatter. When we reached the roped entrance to Kale, the bouncer smiled as if we'd arrived solely to cheer him up.

'Ladies, you are very welcome tonight,' he said. 'Too many men inside. You'll balance out the room nicely.' He unhooked the tatty velvet rope from its brass stand and waved us through, bowing as if he were a gentleman escort instead of a huge bull of a man who could move and punch at terrifying speed. 'Here, on the house for you lovely ladies.' He handed me a wad of drink tickets. Once we were inside I shared them out among the girls and we fanned out through the room carrying our fancy coloured cocktails.

One wall of the bar had railway booths with sliding doors and benches either side of a fixed table. Heavy iron lamps, slung just above head height, gave out a dim yellow light. I slid onto a bench in one of the booths. Shannon moved toward the opposite bench but I asked her to sit beside me. Bree and Ozlem perched on stools at the bar, and Emma and Lu had chosen a round table on the far side of the room. In the gloom, the only way I could recognise our girls at the distant table was Lu's silver sequinned top catching the faint light and rippling like a fish flank in dark water.

You never know who will come up and talk to you at these places, or why. Sometimes they pick demure Shannon, sometimes they're drawn to the party girls like Lu, sometimes a guy will even turn to me, maybe because I look somewhere in between, the underconfident one, the one who might be grateful.

I couldn't sense the necessary hard urgency in the first boys who came to chat us up. They were anxious, skittish, too conscious of their looks and unsure of what to talk about. I could read where things would go because I knew the opening lines so well, the angles they used, the uncomfortable way they leaned on the doorway and kicked restlessly at the baseboard of the booth. Shannon looked pointedly at her phone a couple of times until they took the hint and drifted away.

The next two boys who sidled up to our booth loitered at the carriage door for a few seconds before offering to buy us drinks. We invited them to sit down. They edged in and shifted around until their bodies settled into an awkward stasis. The boy opposite me, tall and skinny, had twisted so far over his drink that he had to look at me with one eye, like a bird, and even then it was through a flop of clean private-school hair. His friend was jiggling his left leg so hard the whole booth shuddered along with it.

At eleven, after we'd got rid of those two and had a drink with a lone boy who quickly lost interest in our conversation and wandered back to his friends at the bar, we decided to leave.

'I parked in the station carpark,' Shannon said. We hurried along the street, heels clattering on the empty footpath, shivering in the cold that had descended in a chill mist while we were inside. My new shoes were rubbing my small toe. I could feel moisture there, perhaps a broken blister or a smear of blood from the chafing, and I thought again of Suze passing the entrance exam for medicine.

'It makes it seem like everything will be all right, doesn't it?' I said to Shannon. 'Now that Suze will be a doctor, I mean.'

'Yeah, it does feel like that.'

The streetlights were blurry in the mist, and the shops we passed were as dark as if they were hung with blackout curtains. The street with its wide verandahs stretched ahead in an overhung corridor of shadow, but no one had followed us from the bar, so we had no reason to be afraid. The only thing to make us hurry was the cold. At the carpark

Shannon beeped open the lock of the Honda. We flung our bags inside and jumped in, and Shannon started the engine so the heater would come on.

'Guess what? I thought ahead.' Shannon leaned over to the back seat and pulled a big canvas bag onto her lap. She extracted a thermos and two white melamine cups from the bag. 'Hot chocolate and there's real chocolate as well. A block of organic dark. I don't know why I never thought of this before.'

'You are brilliant, Shann.'

A couple of times we'd bought hot chips and gravy from the stand in the petrol station on the highway and taken them back to the car, but they had made us feel sick. They'd stunk out the car for days.

I looked at my watch. 'Probably not long now anyway. It wasn't much of a crowd.'

Once we'd snuggled into our seats, with the hot chocolate warming our hands and the car windows fogging up, Shannon turned on the radio. The upbeat voice of the DJ brought a skip of happiness into the car. I loved the first song that he played.

'This is "our song", Steve and me.' I laughed, embarrassed. 'How corny is that, having a song.'

'No!' Shannon rested her cup on the dashboard while she broke three squares of chocolate off the block and handed them to me. 'Eat this before it melts. You're a romantic. It's a byoodiful thang.'

'Ha ha.'

'Is Steve okay with you doing this?'

'I told him I'm at a support group for Suze.'

'Well, we are.'

I nodded and slipped my shoe off. It was too dark in the well of the passenger seat to see if I was bleeding. The loud alert of a text coming through on our phones made us both jump.

Bree and Ozlem clear

'I'll do ours.'

I tapped out our message. *Bec and Shannon clear*

'Hope we don't go too late tonight,' Shannon said through a gluey mouthful of chocolate. 'You want any more to drink?'

I shook my head. The warm cocoa was making me sleepy. I pulled out a tissue and wiped away the steam from the windscreen and the passenger side window, and passed the tissue for Shannon to clean her window. She took it but made a mock face of dismay.

'I quite like the foggy windows. When you can't see out it's like you're in a strange tiny world, car world. Cheap upholstery and farty-smell world.'

'I haven't farted, and if you're going to then please let me know beforehand.'

'Like when people fart in lifts and there's no escape.'

Another text came through, this time from Lu. *Emma and I have split. I am clear.*

'Oh shit, shit. This could be it.' Shannon's voice was wobbly. She grabbed the cup from my hand, opened her driver's door and emptied the contents onto the ground. When she had pulled the door shut she dropped the cups on the floor of the back seat and wiped the driver's side window with the tissue I had passed her.

Another text. *He followed her into Trevvie park. Heading for bridge.*

We reached the park thirty seconds later and got out, trying to close the doors and the boot lid quietly. On our phones, the locate-a-friend app showed Emma in the pagoda beside the pond. Trying to walk fast but quietly made my left shoe chafe even worse and I was certain I was bleeding now. I could feel the moisture seeping into the lining of my shoe and pooling at the toe.

The path through the park was well lit, so we kept to the shadows on the grass, our shoes occasionally crunching stones that had drifted from the white pebbled walkway.

'Shit shit shit,' Shannon hissed. 'We have to turn off the sound on our phones.'

Only a moment after we'd both done that our phones flashed with an incoming text.

Hurry

I pulled off my shoes and started to run down the hill to the bridge that led to the pagoda. My feet ached each time the scattered stones made contact with my tender soles. Shannon, the school athletics champion, sprinted past in the rubber-soled flats she'd slipped on in the car. When I reached the bridge, everyone was there. They turned and looked at me and I understood what they saw in my expression: the rage and fear that had been summoned in me, birthed from the cold sludge pit in my gut of every insult and shaming my friends and I had endured in our short lives. For this moment I was the leader.

We ran silently to the pagoda, where we could see Emma pressed against a pillar, squirming against the grip of a boy who was using his right arm to pin her hands above her head.

'We're here, Emma,' I said. In the darkness my quiet voice seemed to travel along the earth and up through the foundations of the pagoda, flinging the boy backward, away from Emma. As he swung around he stumbled on the uneven flooring and fell to his hands and knees.

'What the hell?' the boy said, but when he raised his face we saw that he wasn't a boy. He was a man in his thirties, or even forties. His pants were undone and his half-erect cock glistened with a droplet of clear liquid at its tip. When he saw us looking he hurriedly stuffed it back into his pants and did up his fly. 'Ladies,' he said, rising on his knees like a begging dog and lifting his hands in a gesture of surrender. 'No harm done here, ladies. We were just having a good time.'

'No,' Emma said. She hitched up her stripy pantyhose, which had been tugged halfway down her thighs, and struggled with her dress until it fell back down into shape. 'No, we weren't, you fucker.'

'Did he say it?' I asked.

Emma shook her head. 'No. You should have waited, like we said. I was okay.'

191

'Say what?' the man said. He was still kneeling. He had nowhere to go. We were all inside the pagoda now. Six women. One man. One baseball bat. 'Look, I wasn't going to rape her or anything. She never said no.' He reached out to Emma. 'You never said no, right?' When his hand touched Emma's thigh the sludge inside me churned up a dim memory of my childhood bedroom and the suffocating weight of the bedclothes. Then the sensation lifted and the clean air of the park flowed over me.

'I never said yes, fucker. I was struggling,' Emma said.

'Show me your face,' I ordered the man.

He turned away. 'No. Why?'

I called Suze on my phone. 'We've got one.'

Lu bent down and thrust her phone toward the man's face. There was a flash. 'Got it. I'm sending now,' Lu said, pressing the button.

Suze's voice was a whisper. 'Did he say it?'

'No, but he mightn't have had time. Lu's sent you a pic.' I could hear the beep as the man's photo arrived on Suze's phone. Things were shifting inside me, again.

'It's not him,' Suze said.

I'll never get it out of my head, what I saw when I found Suze that morning. Two other people, the ones who found the two girls before her, probably have nightmares like me. Three months later, I saw Suze in another way I can never forget, her grey broken face in the hospital after they had pumped her stomach.

He's around here somewhere. This is his patch.

Shannon tsked. 'Oh well, never mind. We seem to have found ourselves a right arsehole though. Baseball, anyone?' She's always had a wicked sense of humour. She swung the bat twice, hard, and it whished through the cold night air like a blade. The kneeling man bowed his head. He was probably praying.

'Do you like baseball?' Shannon asked. As she poked him hard in the back with the bat we all moved in a little closer, our moonshadows stretching and reshaping around us.

'It was a misunderstanding,' he muttered.

She pressed the bat into his shoulder and gave a swift push so that he toppled sideways, flailing his arms.

We looked to Emma, who shrugged.

'Next time,' she said.

The man leaped up and ran off toward the trees.

The breath from our mouths was turning to frost but I wasn't cold anymore. I bent and ran my finger through the blood on my foot then used it to draw a cross on the pillar.

'Next time,' I repeated.

To my surprise Emma laughed, which made me and the others start to laugh. Soon we were laughing so hard that the park filled up with sound, and the whole of the night belonged to us.

Fireworks Night

On the night of the fireworks he rests his hand on the back of my neck as we walk. His hand is heavy and tanned brown. I can picture it lying dark against my neck, the fingers stretched enough to curl around my neck where it meets my shoulder, to cup the rosy hot skin burned by the sun of the summer festival.

We are part of a crowd walking slowly down to the riverbank to watch the fireworks. People smile at me as they pass. They smile because I am not one of them, but I have come to watch anyway. I can appreciate this part of their culture, even though I am a foreigner. I can be a part of this event. We will all be a part of this event, it is for sharing, and we will come away happy and tired and then I will go home. Home to my own country. Tomorrow I will board a plane and go home and one day soon I will share this pleasure with my own people by showing them photographs and telling them about my adventures, and we will all understand each other better. That, I think, is what they believe.

The weight of the brown hand resting on the back of my neck lifts, and Hiroshi points to a stall by the side of the road selling dinner boxes packed with noodles and dumplings and other small delicacies with rice. The stall is lit up by bare bulbs. Plastic flags in red and white stripes hang in an arc from the poles at each corner. The flags flutter in the evening breeze. The breeze and the moving flags make it seem like it should be cool, but it is still hot, the air is dank with humidity, and Hiroshi's warm hand has left a moist print on the back of my neck. He reaches around my waist and guides me toward the stall, where the stallholder is shouting a welcome and waving his tongs over the range of his merchandise. I am wearing a black rayon dress that hangs from two thin straps at my shoulders. Hiroshi's hand is hot through the rayon of my black dress as though we were skin to skin.

'*Irasshai!*' the stallholder shouts. 'Welcome, hallo! Hallo Miss America!'

He has a row of golden teeth along the bottom of his jaw that gleam in the light of the bare bulbs. At the stall next door, a man is selling goldfish to children. His stall is a series of plastic blue and white pools teeming with fish. The children have to scoop up a fish in a tiny net, then they are given their catch in a plastic bag filled with water. The fish man waves a scooping net at me, 'Hallo, fish here, hallo.' The golden-toothed stallholder makes a joke in a low voice to the fish man and they both laugh before turning away from me and Hiroshi.

'What did they say?' I ask Hiroshi, and he looks at me. I can see his lips moving as he tries to form the translation in his mouth, but his mouth is all slow and sticky from the heat and he cannot make the English from the Japanese.

'About fish,' Hiroshi says, and shrugs. Translating is too much trouble – it is too hot.

A small child wearing a Japanese happi coat and tiny wooden sandals clatters past and touches my sleeve on the way.

'Hallo, hallo, sensei,' she calls before her mother puts a hand on the small of her back and pushes her forward.

I know this child, although I can't remember her name. 'Hallo,' I call back. 'Goodbye.'

She came to my class a few times, my class of toddlers and young children who repeated English words after me so accurately that I could hear my own Australian accent in their voices. *To die is choose die. What will we do to die?* The mother looks back over her shoulder and nods her head slightly as she smiles to me.

Further along the road, a few stalls selling grilled chicken skewers have set up. The fat from the chicken drips and sizzles on the coals and the aroma wafts along the street past us. Two businessmen, their ties loosened and their sleeves rolled up, sit on low stools in front of the closest stall, drinking from big mugs of beer.

We pass the local supermarket with its bargain bins of socks and cabbages, then the futon shop. Fluffy futons are stacked five high on pallets out the front while the old man who owns the shop sits drinking tea on tatami matting inside the window. He stares at me and Hiroshi as we stroll by, as if he thinks the window makes him invisible. Further along the road the pottery shop owner pulls down her shutter, locks it, then joins the crowd moving toward the river. Watching her brush streaks of clay dust from her shirt as she walks, I realise that the sights on this walk are souvenirs I should be collecting.

Hiroshi is swinging the plastic bag with our dinner boxes back and forth in time with our steps. He leans over and takes my hand in his, then lifts it to his mouth and blows cool air into my palm.

'Hot night,' he says, then laughs. 'Hot August night.'

At home, August is the month when we have lost patience with the cold and the dark. We long for nights like this.

As we round a corner on the road we see the riverbank laid out before us like a woodblock print. Many hundreds of people are gathered to watch the fireworks. They sit in groups, their brightly coloured cotton kimonos glowing in the dusk light. Each group has its own patchwork of ground-sheets and blankets, and pairs of shoes and sandals are lined up neatly at the edge of each group's territory. Paper lanterns sway on the decks of flat-bottomed boats cruising up and down the river, and down by the dock a man with a mega-phone tries to organise a group of unruly elderly citizens.

I feel a rush of panic for what I am about to lose. I stop for a moment and breathe in deeply, trying to capture and hold the complicated scent that is Tokyo on a hot summer night.

We pick our way among the parties on the riverbank and find a small spot to spread our plastic sheet. I slip off my sandals and step onto the plastic. Hiroshi passes me the dinner boxes and I hold them while he unlaces his shoes and pulls off his socks, then steps onto the sheet beside me. As I look down I glimpse where my dress strap has slipped. The white skin where I was protected by the dress stands out in stark contrast to my pink shoulders and arms, as though this day, this festival, this country has burned its impression onto my body. I will never belong here and yet this place has become a part of me. A part that for the rest of my life will ache when I least expect it.

Just as we have opened our boxes and lifted salty pickled plums to our mouths, the first firework explodes above us. Then another and another and for half an hour we all stare upward at the brilliant light of the sky, and at the climax the whole sky burns bright until suddenly there is only darkness and the smell of the burned powder and empty bottles and dinner boxes and children asleep on their parents' shoulders and it is over.

Acknowledgments

To my Kanzaman friends, Jane Watson, Mary Manning, Penny Gibson, Pam Baker and Janey Runci, thank you for your helpful comments on story drafts and your excellent company. To all the literary magazines, thank you for being the engines of the short story world. And to Madonna Duffy, thank you for having me on your wonderful list.

Publication details

'The Salesman', *Griffith REVIEW 29: Prosper or Perish*, 2010; and *The Best Australian Stories 2010*, ed. Cate Kennedy, Black Inc., 2010.

'Procession', *Going Down Swinging*, Issue 30, 2010.

'The City Circle', *Griffith REVIEW 45: The Way We Work*, 2014.

'Stingers', *Review of Australian Fiction*, Volume 10, Issue 6, 2014.

'After the Goths', *Readings and Writings: Forty Years in Books*, eds Jason Cotter and Michael Williams, Hardie Grant, 2009.

'Family Reunion', published as 'The Good Son', *Australian Book Review*, June 2009.

'The Word', *Southerly*, Volume 68, Number 2, 2008.

'One Good Thing', *Brothers and Sisters*, ed. Charlotte Wood, Allen & Unwin, 2009.

'Breaking Up', *Overland*, Issue 192, 2008; and *New Australian Stories*, ed. Aviva Tuffield, Scribe, 2009.

'Serenity Prayer', published as 'Reality TV', *The Great Unknown*, ed. Angela Meyer, Spineless Wonders, 2013.

'Territory', published as 'Friday Nights', *Review of Australian Fiction*, Volume 4, Issue 2, 2012.

'Fireworks Night', *Eureka Street*, 12 March 2008.

Also by Paddy O'Reilly
THE END OF THE WORLD

A sparkling collection of award-winning stories.

Stylistically varied and enlivened by a wry, dark humour, the stories in this collection span a broad range of experience – an alien visitor who communicates in the language of romance, a woman waiting for her death, a case of confused identity, and the sour taste of relationships lost or abandoned.

O'Reilly's characters are at once defiant and accepting, curious and bewildered. From Japan to suburban Australia, and onto a place where larger, odder things are possible, *The End of the World* plays with our perceptions of reality.

'Fresh on every page, adventurous, enlightening, nicely restrained yet vivid and often moving.' *Australian*

ISBN 978 0 7022 3594 8

Lightning Source UK Ltd.
Milton Keynes UK
UKOW06f2003190715

255409UK00017B/328/P

9 780702 253607